5-04

P9-BYI-659

DATE DUE NH LS X

JUN 1 ~~AUG~~ ~~0143~~ ~~2010~~	JUN 15 2012		
JUL 01 2004			
~~JUL~~ ~~13~~ ~~2004~~			
JUL 30 2004			
AUG 27 2004			
SEP 10 2004			
SEP 08 2006			
JUN 18 2009			

MT

THIS
TIME LOVE

Other books by Tara Randel:

Melody of Love
Hidden Hearts
Lasting Love

THIS
TIME LOVE

•

Tara Randel

AVALON BOOKS
NEW YORK

PRINTED IN THE UNITED STATES OF AMERICA
ON ACID-FREE PAPER
BY HADDON CRAFTSMEN, BLOOMSBURG, PENNSYLVANIA

To my parents, William and Dorothy Donovan,
for teaching me the importance of family.
I love you.

Chapter One

If you want custody of your niece, you'll have to get married first.

Lindsey Summer stood alone in her grandmother's living room, stunned beyond belief by her sister's melodramatic ultimatum. Her sister couldn't be serious, could she? Was this just another whim? *Marriage to keep Risa from taking Dawn away?*

Clamping her lips together, Lindsey moved to stare out the window. It wasn't that Lindsey didn't want to get married. She'd come close once. Risa knew this, but yet she'd come up with this crazy idea, knowing full well the upheaval her demand would cause in Lindsey's life. And who would she marry anyway? She wasn't even dating anyone right now. Talk about your double whammy.

Risa had never been a true mother to the girl. Lindsey had filled that spot in Dawn's life. No matter how many times Risa came home, full of vague promises and excuses for her vagabond lifestyle, she still wouldn't do the one thing that would make Lindsey's life complete—allow Lindsey to have legal custody of Dawn as her daughter.

Friends had suggested to Lindsey that she sue for custody, but since Risa wasn't abusive and hadn't abandoned Dawn, the family had decided not to pursue legal action against her and hoped Risa would change her ways. So far, that hadn't happened.

Briskly rubbing her hands up and down her arms, Lindsey paced the room. Something wasn't right here. Normally Risa would march right into their lives, make a play at being a mother, then leave town with the next available guy promising to show her a good time. This time she seemed different, unsettled almost, but still skillfully managed to leave the entire family anxious and bickering.

And this made Lindsey extremely nervous.

The door eased open. Dawn stepped into the living room, her eyes wide with concern. "Hey, Mom."

Lindsey spied Dawn hovering at the door. Her heart grew lighter and she smiled. At about five years old, Dawn had started calling Lindsey "Mom." When she grew older, she realized Risa was her birth mother, but refused to call her so. As far as Dawn was concerned, Lindsey was her mother.

Dawn hurried over to Lindsey, much too serious and somber for an 11 year old. "Risa left a few minutes ago. Said she'd be back in a few days." Dawn chewed on her lower lip before asking, "Why does she always come here and make you sad?"

Lindsey hugged her into a tight embrace, breathing in the scent of this beloved niece, who was as close to the only child as she'd ever get. "She doesn't make me sad. Risa is . . . hard to understand. Even if she has ideas that are a bit unconventional, she means well."

I think.

Dawn pulled from the embrace. "This time she seemed serious."

"I noticed that too."

"I don't want her to take me away. I love living with you. I can't imagine being anywhere else."

Lindsey couldn't imagine it either. Only a few hours earlier she was sitting on the couch, correcting papers, in the cozy cottage she and Dawn shared and the next thing she knew, Risa showed up and demanded a family meeting at Gramma's house. Lindsey still struggled to make sense of it all.

"I don't think we should get too worried yet. Risa's up to something, but I don't think she'd just up and take you with her. After all, you have school and soccer."

"And Em."

Lindsey grinned at the mention of Dawn's best friend.

"And Em."

"She called a few minutes ago to ask if I could come over. Her dad promised to make some kinda special dinner, tacos I think, and she's all excited."

"I thought maybe we could hang out tonight. In case you wanted to talk."

Dawn rolled her eyes. "I know that Risa's visit has upset everyone. That's why I kinda wanted to get away for a while."

Lindsey took a deep breath. How well she knew that feeling.

But Dawn was right, she needed a night away from the drama. And if anyone could make her niece happy, it was Emily Banner.

"Besides," Dawn argued, "my math grade isn't too good, but Em's been helping me and I think I can do better."

Lindsey loosely held Dawn an arm's length away. "You can't fool me. You're fine in math."

Dawn shrugged and grinned. "Okay. But I really want to go."

"All right. I suppose we can put off our hanging out together until another time."

Dawn circled Lindsey's waist with her skinny arms and hugged her close. "Thanks." After a quick squeeze, she turned for the door. "Papa said he'd drive me."

Lindsey silently thanked her father for volunteering. She'd need some time to unwind before she got behind the wheel of a car. "I'll pick you up at eight."

"When you come to get me, could you, um, change into something a little more . . . fancy?"

Lindsey looked down at her favorite worn blue jeans and oversized pink sweater. Since when had this 11 year old turned into the fashion police? "What's wrong with my outfit?"

"Nothing," Dawn frantically assured her. "It's just that, maybe you could at least put on a prettier top."

Lindsey frowned at Dawn's conspiratorial expression. "If you think that by dressing up I'll catch Mr. Banner's eye—"

"No, that's not it at all."

Lindsey could almost hear the gears grinding in Dawn's mind.

"I just thought you could wear that embroidered blouse I gave you for Christmas."

Biting back a smile, Lindsey used her best authoritative voice to confront her niece. "Dawn Marie Summer, no matchmaking."

Dawn's eyes lit up in surprise. "Me? No way. I'd never do that."

Lindsey suspiciously raised an eyebrow, the way she always did when questioning her niece's motives.

"Okay," Dawn relented. "I'd never do it if you didn't want me to. I mean, if you don't know, that's one thing.

But you seem interested in Mr. Banner so I thought maybe you could impress him."

Lindsey silently balked at having this adult conversation with a mere child. A child a little too intuitive for her own good. "I'm not interested in Mr. Banner. The fact that your best friend Emily is my student is the only form of relationship I have with him."

Sure, sure. Then why does my heart beat a little faster when someone mentions his name? Or when I see him, however briefly, around town?

Dawn looked confused. "But he told Em that you both knew each other growing up."

He'd actually spoke about her? Surprised by the sudden information, she tried not to appear the least bit affected.

"We did. But that was a long time ago."

"Oh." Dawn's voice grew solemn. "Are you upset with me?"

"Never," Lindsey assured her, taking her in one last embrace before letting the young girl go. "Never." She tugged on a lock of Dawn's soft tawny hair. "Go. Have fun."

"See ya." Dawn's voice echoed as she streaked down the hallway.

"Yeah, see ya." Lindsey sighed. Not only would she sit here contemplating her uncertain future, now she had the possible meeting up with Gabe Banner to fret over. He'd been back in town for six months now, and she'd only had a couple of run-ins with him because he had traveled back and forth to Florida to finish up his law cases. When she did see him, she still got that spine-tingling thrill when she was anywhere near the man. As much as she'd want to walk down memory lane with Gabe, his daughter was one of her students. She had to present a professional front, despite the fact that her heart melted whenever she saw him. No man had ever had such a pleasurable effect on her. He seemed friendly, but they hadn't been able to talk long enough to see if the attraction was mutual. And if it was, where it might lead.

And knowing Dawn and her propensity for curiosity, Lindsey didn't want to divulge any juicy details about her past with Gabe, especially with the way things had turned out. It was bad enough that the note she'd sent him during their senior year in high school had changed their lives. She didn't want to dwell on the past.

Wandering back to the window, she felt the teenage angst slip away as she took solace in the mountain view spreading majestically before her eyes. Spring was upon them, bringing renewed life to the north Georgia mountains. She cherished these warmer days. The lingering scent of blooming hyacinths scented the air. Sunny daffodils popped their yellow blooms through the sleeping ground, bringing riots of bright color to the once dreary landscape. Her grandmother's gardens, now teeming with crocus and tulips amid the natural landscaping, caused annual envy from every would-be horticulturist in town.

Right now she stood in her grandparents' home, a weathered, two-story farmhouse, complete with a welcoming front porch. On the same property and all within walking distance, were also her parents' log cabin, two barns, and nestled into the side of the mountain, her own cottage. The entire property had become affectionately known as "the compound."

Lindsey had lived in the cottage, originally built for Risa, who had never taken up residence, for five years. Along with Dawn. She'd heard the stories for years, how Lindsey's great-grandfather originally settled on the property, adding the farmhouse when Granddaddy married. Then he built a rustic log cabin house for Daddy. And on and on and on . . . They weren't all within sneezing distance, but sometimes it felt pretty darn close.

Most folks in the county thought the idea of all the Summer family members living in close proximity to each other as quaint. Lindsey found it trying at times, but right now it was a necessity. Risa needed to see that Dawn had stability, that Risa's mobile lifestyle was no way of life for a smart young girl. And with the other family members close by, Risa conceded that Dawn had a good, safe life here. Dawn relied on Lindsey for maternal support, but Lindsey needed Dawn just as much.

As a young adult, Lindsey had been diagnosed with endometriosis. Not life threatening, but the doctor informed her that the odds were against her ever having children. To do so would be a miracle.

In her heart of hearts, Lindsey knew Dawn was that miracle. Dawn belonged in her life, for now and always.

So now, Risa brought the conflict most dreaded to Lindsey's heart. Risa wanted, no, demanded, that Lindsey marry, but most of the men Lindsey had dated wanted children. Even her college fiancé had broken off the engagement when Lindsey confided to him that children with her would be impossible. His reaction had nearly broken her heart. How on earth did her sister expect her to find a man who would accept her as she was? She couldn't face that soul-searing rejection again. She had to convince Risa that this was a bad plan.

A slight movement on the fringes of the woods caught Lindsey's attention. A small animal, a rabbit maybe, scampering around in search of food. Lindsey smiled. She knew the foot-worn trails on the property like the back of her hand. In fact, she knew just about everyone in town, as well, especially the children who had been her students the past five years. She moved her gaze from the tiny rabbit to the high, sprawling mountains in the backdrop. The mountains that held a special magic for her, gave her a sense of peace.

But now her entire future hung suspended in a dimension of worry and fear, brought on by her older sister. Risa had always been unfairly demanding, even when she lived at home, wanting things her way or no way, no matter the cost or who she hurt. Over the years she'd hurt the family plenty, especially when she turned her back on them and up and married a young man who was passing through town, then became pregnant. And when her hasty marriage quickly ended, she expected the family to raise her child. Which they did, no questions asked.

If you want custody of Dawn, you'll have to get married.

Lindsey tried to be patient because she understood Risa's troubled childhood, but this newest demand from her sister came as a total surprise to Lindsey. How far would she go to make good on her sister's demand? Would Risa really uproot her daughter from the only life she'd ever known to live a life on the road? Dawn deserved better than that. Would Lindsey have to prepare for battle, a legal battle if necessary, since Risa changed the unspoken rules that had guided them for years?

Get married? Her spirits sank as she considered the ultimatum again. How could Risa make such a demand? What was going on in her life that she would do this? Of course, if Lindsey waited long enough, Risa might change her mind. She had done so before with some of her demands. But a niggling sense of uncertainty bothered Lindsey. Did Risa think that at 30, since Lindsey was having difficulty getting a man, she would try to change that by way of ultimatum?

Lindsey had her reasons for not dating—she couldn't deal with the disappointment of knowing she wouldn't have children. So Dawn and her students filled that gap in her life. Risa knew that, so what was she trying to pull?

In retrospect, even her college fiancé hadn't been the man for her. Numbed by that heartache, Lindsey realized that she might never find her Mr. Right. As far as she was concerned, the only man who'd ever come close had eloped and left town years ago, with his wife, a friend Lindsey had trusted and been betrayed by. Later, Lindsey learned that they'd had a child of their own.

Maybe that's why she'd clung all these years to the thought of becoming Dawn's mother. To having that connection that would elude her otherwise.

"Honey, are you okay?"

Lindsey turned at the sound of her mother's voice, wishing she didn't feel so pitiful.

"Honestly Mom? I don't know."

Laurel Ann Summer floated across the room, her purple, sparkly gauze blouse and flowing skirt billowing around her ankles, her many bracelets tinkling like the musical melody of a wind chime. She took a seat on the worn, comfortable couch. Her still beautiful model's face showed little of the worry over Risa that Lindsey knew she hid from the world. "I don't suppose she'll come back with a change of heart over this marriage contingency?"

Lindsey joined her mother on the opposite end of the sofa, tucking her legs under her. "I'm not holding my breath."

"I wonder where she came up with this latest idea?"

"There's no telling. I've never been able to figure out the way she thinks."

Laurel Ann let out a long-suffering sigh. "I guess we've enabled her behavior all these years. Maybe we're to blame for this latest escapade."

Lindsey watched her mother close her eyes, catching no

glimpse of any new, minute wrinkles on her still-famous face. It seemed that her mother never aged. With her trademark facial creams and lotions, she remained a walking advertisement for Laurel Ann Skinmetics and her products. Risa had inherited her mother's gorgeous blond hair, and willowy figure, while Lindsey resembled her father's side of the family with loose, loopy black curls and an outdoorsey complexion. Sturdy good looks, her grandmother told her. Plain and unglamourous, Lindsey told herself. She could stand to lose five pounds—okay, seven—but who was counting anyway?

Hey, she knew genes were a luck of the draw, but every once in a while she wished she'd gotten more of what her mom had.

Living here on the family compound had taught Lindsey to rely on her abilities, not her outward appearance. She'd dreamed of being a teacher and she now taught fifth grade at Paineville Elementary. She wanted to fight against illiteracy, so she held a seat on the library board and had started the first literacy outreach program in the community. It became so successful, it had been adopted in the surrounding communities. She usually attained her goals, with the exception of getting full custody of Dawn. And now her sister had made that more difficult than ever.

"We both know Risa's track record for her antics. I'm thinking maybe I should just play along until she changes her mind, which, knowing Risa, is extremely probable."

The two women sat deep in thought in the quiet, homey living room her grandmother had created. Potpourri scented the house, lace curtains framed large windows, and pinewood floors shined with welcome. The well-worn furnishings that surrounded Lindsey and her mother provided a comfortable atmosphere for hours of conversation. Risa had almost ruined that haven earlier today with her impromptu meeting in this very room.

"You know what is so ironic?" her mother said. "Here we are actually considering this hare-brained scheme that Risa hatched up, and *she's* the unpredictable one."

Lindsey chuckled, then scooted closer to the center of the couch. "Okay, so I play along with this. Maybe it'll satisfy her to see me act as though I'm really looking. But how on earth am I supposed to find a husband? I'm not even dating anyone."

"Which I've been trying to remedy for some time now."

"Mom!"

She held up her palm. "I'm just saying, you've wasted precious time by not pursuing a man. You're not getting any younger, you know."

Her mother's own personal demon.

"I haven't been . . . interested." She left it at that.

"Why not? Because none of the men have been Gabe Banner?"

Lindsey's jaw dropped in shock. So now she'd have to answer to her mother? Whose side was she on, anyway?

But she heard the frustration in her mother's tone and softened. Her mother had never completely forgiven Gabe for breaking her daughter's heart. How could she, when Lindsey had cried on her mother's shoulder for hours all those years ago.

When the memory struck, Lindsey fought back a sudden wave of longing. Senior year of high school, Gabe had seemed genuinely interested in her. If he hadn't, she never would have thought about sending that note, asking him to meet her in the park so they could talk. Instead, Cindy had learned about Lindsey's idea to send the note, written her own and Gabe had ended up meeting with her. Lindsey's

Mr. Right had left, only recently to return as a widower and single father.

She hoped her mother didn't notice the slight quiver in her voice when she lied. "Gabe Banner? Mom, that's ridiculous. I've been over him for years."

"Have you? Then why are you avoiding him? Why haven't you gotten together with Gabe and Emily? Dawn's always asking you to do things with them, but you always have an excuse."

"They . . . aren't excuses." Lindsey stumbled over her words. "I have legitimate things to do."

And legitimate reasons for staying away.

"Such as?" Her mother raised a perfectly plucked eyebrow in suspicion.

Lindsey racked her brain to come up with an answer. "The library. Oh, and school. Watching out for Gramma and Granddaddy, which is a full time job—"

"Excuses."

"Excuses for what?"

"For hiding out in your cottage."

Lindsey crossed her arms over her chest. "So what do you propose I do?"

"Get out there and date. There are plenty of men in this town alone interested in you. You just send off the wrong signals, so they won't approach you. I've had a few men actually ask about you."

Lindsey gasped, appalled. "What men? Where?"

"Ron Silva for one. I saw him at the General Store last week and he asked about you. In fact, we talked about you for a good half hour."

"Really?" She frowned. "Ron?" Fussy, workaholic Ron?

"Then there was Jerry Richmond. He cornered me after church one Sunday, asking me if you were going to attend the pot luck. He was very disappointed when you decided to stay home and grade book reports."

"I thought he was dating Tina."

"They broke up. He was upset, but he's looking now."

Great. Now she'd be a rebound date.

"I don't know," she hedged.

"Of course, you don't know. You've gone into hiding even more since Gabe came back to town."

Lindsey tried to hide the fact that Gabe's presence in town had her all turned around. "No, I—"

"Yes," her mother told her, directly and distinctly. She pointed a red enameled fingernail at her. "You have."

"No." Lindsey remained adamant, not wanting to give her mother any ammunition to use against her. Memories of Gabe were special to her and she meant to keep it that way.

"All right then, prove he doesn't mean anything to you," she challenged. "Go out and date other men instead of hiding."

Her mother's words slowly sank in. Had she really been hiding? Maybe. But not consciously.

"You have a major dilemma here," her mother continued. "If you don't date, it doesn't look to Risa like you're trying to find a husband. If you don't look like you're pursuing a husband, you don't get custody of Dawn."

"It just feels so . . . mercenary."

"Mercenary. Necessary. What's the difference?"

Lindsey looked at her mother's expression and her already sagging spirits dropped even lower. She had that I'll-fix-everything-dear glint in her eyes. And Lindsey knew what that meant. Another makeover, for one. More advice than she needed or wanted, for two. And, ultimately, a long challenge ahead of her, for three.

Great, her mother didn't need much encouragement to set her up with eligible men and Risa's plan fed right into her dating machinations.

Nothing good could come of this.

"You have a choice to make. Either start dating in search of a husband or lose Dawn."

"There's no choice to make. I won't lose Dawn."

"Then it's settled. You'll make yourself more visible around town. Go to some of the church outings. Make it known that you want to date." Her mother smiled and spoke the worst sentence in the English language. "Before you go public, I suggest a *makeover*."

Lindsey shuddered.

"Let me blow out your curls. Your hair is lovely when we can keep it straight. And, the R&D department of Laurel Ann Skinmetics just sent me a whole new eye shadow selection that would be perfect with your coloring."

Lindsey closed her eyes and cringed at the thought. *Remember, you're doing this for Dawn. For Dawn.*

Laurel Ann had stopped speaking, so Lindsey slitted her eyes open, glancing at her mother. A patent look of disapproval crossed the woman's face.

"Are you listening to me?"

"Yes, I am." Lindsey took a bracing breath. "When do we begin?"

Chapter Two

Two hours, and a complete makeover later, Lindsey stood on the doorstep of Gabe Banner's home. Well, not his house, exactly. His grandmother, Ruby Sue Callahan, actually owned it. Lindsey was reminded of this often because Dawn was a walking statistician concerning the Banner family. She could recite the family history, verbatim, as told to her by Emily.

Let's see if she remembered correctly. Gabe and Emily had moved in with Ruby Sue when they moved back to Paineville. He was currently working construction with his older brother, Ty, whose wife Casey was expecting a baby in a few months. Gabe's sister, Marilyn, had gotten married to the famous music writer, Dusty Haywood, last Christmas.

Lindsey chuckled over Dawn's dissertation of the Banner family. She rang the doorbell, nervously running her fingers through her now straight hair, courtesy of her mother, and smoothed the sleeves on her red embroidered blouse. The one Dawn had given her for Christmas. The one Lindsey couldn't believe she'd actually changed into to pick up her niece. Her mother had actually given her fashion blessing, saying the Blue Paradise eye shadow choice went well with Lindsey's eyes.

The door opened and bright light spilled out as Gabe Banner filled the doorway, one eyebrow lifted over smokey grey eyes. His tall, wide shoulders admirably filled out his T-shirt, nearly spanning the width of the open space. His broken-in jeans looked worn and comfortable. She swallowed hard as she considered the masculine package he presented. Construction work definitely agreed with him.

"Hi. I'm here to pick up Dawn."

"Lindsey. C'mon in. The girls are upstairs."

He moved back and motioned for her to enter. As she stepped over the threshold, she brushed by him. Not much, but enough for her arm to tingle and her heart to skip double time. Once inside the foyer she faced him, blinking a few times as she stared up into his cool gaze. His dark brown hair needed a cut, she noticed, while his fabulous eyes, locked with hers, held a hint of humor. For a moment she forgot to breathe, then mentally shook herself. She didn't come here to ogle the man. She came here to pick up Dawn. She'd do well to remember that small fact.

"So, how have you been?" he asked, casually leaning against the carved wooden post at the bottom of the stairway, his strong arms crossed over his impressive chest.

"Fine. Just great. Um, things are good. Fine. Fine." *Stop blabbering.*

He grinned. A devastating combination of humor and good looks. "Glad to hear it."

"And you?"

"Fine. Just great."

His husky tone held a hint of promise. The kind of promise a woman longed to hear on a candle-lit, romantic night.

She licked her suddenly dry lips and shifted on one hip to assure a casual stance. "So, is Dawn ready?"

His eyes flickered to the movement of her lips, then back up to her gaze. Before he could answer her, Ruby Sue, the family matriarch, appeared at the top of the stairs.

"She'll be done in a minute," Ruby Sue informed them as she came down the stairs. "They're cleaning up Emily's room."

The older woman beamed at Lindsey, then Gabe, and back to Lindsey. She grinned from ear to ear. Knowing full well how Ruby Sue operated with her matchmaking schemes, Lindsey parted her lips to speak. Too late, Ruby Sue beat her to it.

"How have you been, Lindsey? Haven't seen you about town much lately." She turned to Gabe, not giving Lindsey an opening to answer. "Why don't you take Lindsey into the parlor. You two take a seat while I fetch some tea. It's still kinda cool outside for beginning of April, though the almanac says we should have a real warming spell soon."

"Thank you, but I really should—"

"It'll just take me a minute. Gabe, go on now, show our guest into the other room." The woman shuffled off to the kitchen, pretending not to hear Lindsey's protest.

Lindsey glanced at Gabe, trying to read his reaction to his grandmother's command. "I really don't want to impose. I just wanted to get Dawn and leave."

Gabe shrugged casually, the movement revealing his humor. "Don't fight it. If Gran wants you to have tea, she'll make sure we have tea. Let's go take a seat."

Lindsey followed him into the warm parlor, perching on one of the two wingback chairs flanking the couch. Gabe took the other, his quiet gaze assessing her. She felt herself growing warm under his intense scrutiny, but somehow didn't feel uncomfortable. No, oh no, the heat he sent her way brought out the buried femininity in her. And in the clarity of the moment, she had to admit she hadn't felt this feminine in a long time. Gabe hadn't said more than a handful of words, but he certainly knew how to bring out the woman in her.

"Emily and Dawn seem to have hit it off big time," Gabe commented, his lips quirked in a secret smile.

"I'm so glad about that. Dawn tends to be quiet and withdrawn."

"And Emily is always wide open. She pulls Dawn right along in her wake. They make a good match."

"In school, the two really help each other out," Lindsey assured him. "It's so cute to watch. They're almost as close as sisters."

Gabe stretched out his long legs and crossed them at the ankles. "So, you became a teacher."

"And you a lawyer."

"Not right now. I'm not practicing."

"I'd heard that. So you're working construction with Ty until you get your Georgia license?"

"No. I quit law. Completely."

Lindsey opened her eyes wide. "Really? I thought you loved your practice."

"For a while. It lost it's appeal."

He didn't come out and say it, but Lindsey could almost hear the underlying reason. *Practicing law has lost it's appeal without Cindy here.*

Now feeling completely uncomfortable, Lindsey glanced at the stairs when she heard the racket of feet pounding down the staircase and the non-stop chatter of girls' voices. She sagged with relief, grateful she'd dodged the chance of sharing memories about Cindy with Gabe.

"Hey," she called as the girls scampered into the room. With their similar shade of light brown hair, they almost resembled sisters.

Dawn came to stand beside her. "I'm ready now." Emily jumped up into her daddy's lap.

Lindsey stood and tugged the car keys out of her front pants pocket. "It's getting late, we should go."

"No tea?" Gabe asked.

"Tell your grandmother thanks, but we should run. School tomorrow."

The four walked to the door, Dawn and Emily beaming at each other. They bid their good-byes.

"See you around town," Gabe said in parting, his eyes enigmatic when he spoke. Was he being polite or was there more to his words? She could only hope.

On the ride home, Dawn kept looking at Lindsey, then the embroidered blouse, all the while with a silly grin on her face, giving Lindsey a bad feeling.

"So, you girls have fun tonight?"

"Yep."

"Do anything exciting?"

"Can't tell you."

"And why not?"

"Because you'll get mad."

"No I won't."

"Oh yes, you will."

"Dawn . . ."

"Okay, okay. If you must know, we were planning our family."

"What's that supposed to mean?"

"You heard what Risa told you. You have to get married or she'll take me away."

"So you two were planning my future?"

"Yes. And we have a really good idea."

She had a nagging sense that she knew what Dawn was going to say. "This I have to hear."

"You and Mr. Banner are gonna get married! Then Em and I can be real sisters."

Lindsey nearly drove the car off the road. Her head grew light at the thought of being Gabe's wife. Wouldn't that be a dream come true. Her insides flipped with hope.

"So what do you think?" Dawn asked, her tone serious.

What did she think? Between her mother's dating idea and the girls' family plans, she didn't know what to think. She only knew that life, as she knew it, was over.

As the late morning light filtered into the living room, Gabe Banner meticulously sanded the last section of the banister before he would stain the wood. Deep in thought, he pictured Lindsey standing in the hallway last night and smiled. Ruby Sue hadn't managed to run her off. Not that he was much of a conversationalist, but they'd managed to find out a few things about each other. He hadn't seen her since high school, and since returning to town, he'd been busy finishing up his law cases in Florida and working with Ty. With a small grin, he had to admit, she looked good. Real good.

"Why is it so quiet in here?" Ty Banner asked as he sauntered into the airy foyer they were currently remodeling. "You know I need noise when I'm working."

"Hey, artist working here," Gabe called to his dark-haired brother from his position beside the staircase. "I need to concentrate."

"Yeah, well, it's time for a lunch break." Ty broke into a full grin and held up a large bag. "Courtesy of Casey."

Gabe carefully laid the sanding tool on the floor and

followed his brother into the large living room while Ty fished around in the paper bag.

"Don't keep me in suspense, what did she send us this time?"

"Tomato and mayonnaise sandwiches."

"I haven't had one of those since we were kids."

"Enjoy it. Casey makes the best. Ever since she found out we're going to have a baby, she's gotten real maternal, you know, cooking and decorating the nursery. And she has lots of extra time, especially since cutting down her hours at Crafty Creations." Ty tossed him a wrapped package. "So, we get great food."

Gabe caught the sandwich, then kicked over a wooden crate and took a seat. "Got anything to wash this down with?"

Ty shrugged off his jacket before searching for a soda can in the bag and handed it to him. "Since Casey is pretty much home bound, she's gotten serious about this cooking rivalry she's got going with Ruby Sue. I have to say, every night when I go home, I don't know what to expect for dinner."

"Don't complain. Thank God you've got a wife at home."

"Trust me, bro, I do that every day."

They fell into a silence while they ate. Gabe gazed around the room, pleased with the results of their work so far. The new owners of the house bought this large colonial a few miles out of town and wanted a complete renovation before moving in. Ty had accepted the job in December, so they'd spent a great deal of time indoors working on the plans left by the owners. Gabe had made his final trip to Florida just last month, so now he focused on the job at hand.

He looked around the room and let out a laugh.

"What?" Ty asked before taking a drink from the soda can.

"This place is a far cry from where we grew up."

Ty nodded. "Yeah, it is. But look at us now. I've got a baby on the way. Ruby lives in a big house instead of the cramped trailer all four of us lived in. Marilyn finally found Dusty to settle down with. I didn't think our little sister would ever find a good guy.

"And now you and Emily are home, where you should be." He glanced at Gabe. "Really, when it comes right down to it, we survived all those years growing up because we had each other. Family, man, that's where it's at."

"Can't argue that point. Who else but family would give me a woodworking job when I quit my practice to move back here?"

Gabe had signed on to work with Ty since coming home, so he found himself right in the middle of the job, doing the more specialized job of woodwork; from banisters, to bookcases, and fancy crown molding. As a teenager, he'd worked construction with his brother in the summers and found he really had a knack with wood. This talent had also helped put him through law school. Now he enjoyed it because it was anything but law.

"You know I'd do anything for you," Ty reminded him.

"I know."

"So, as your older brother, I've got to warn you."

Gabe's eyebrow rose. "About?"

Ty took a seat on the floor near Gabe. "I have it on good authority that there are plenty of single women in town ready to fawn all over you. Shoot, look how they went after Dusty when he first came to town. Casey's been dropping hints left and right about who she can set you up with. You're in trouble, man."

Gabe swallowed the last bite of his sandwich. He'd been on a few dates in recent years, mostly staid business-type functions. He didn't want to get hooked up with a party girl. Cindy had started down that path just before she died.

He flashed back to the day Cindy had died. Gabe hadn't liked the crowd Cindy insisted on hanging around with. After years of being an at-home mom, she'd gotten a job as a receptionist in an office complex that shared a central answering service and receptionist as part of the perk of renting office space in the building. Cindy had loved being part of the work force and had taken her socializing time with her co-workers seriously.

On that horrible day, they had a fight. Cindy refused to listen to him and went out . . . where was it now? Oh yeah, a picnic with her friends. He didn't want Em going with her, so he had stayed home with their daughter. Maybe if he hadn't been so stubborn, if he'd been driving, maybe she would have avoided trouble. The thing was, he couldn't know for sure and he couldn't change things. Bottom line, he hadn't been able to help his own wife.

"Hey, bro, where'd you go? You've got that funny look on your face."

Gabe sighed. "Thinking about the day Cindy died."

"Not healthy, man."

"I know. I always wondered if I had been with her, would things have changed."

"Gabe, you loved Cindy. We all know that."

Gabe laughed, not pleasantly. "You know what? I think we were headed toward really serious marital problems. We'd grown apart, had different interests. Jeez, even now I feel guilty thinking about it."

Ty stared back at him, clearly stunned by his brother's news. "Whoa. I never would have guessed."

"That's what living so far from your family does, helps

you hide problems. I'm sure you would have noticed if we lived here."

Ty didn't respond for a while. "Yeah, well, despite all that, you really need to think about dating. Especially in light of our situation with Emily."

Gabe sat up straight. "I didn't realize we had a situation."

Ty rolled his sandwich wrapper into a ball. "Emily needs a mother."

Deep down, Gabe knew that. "It's that obvious?"

"Yeah. So what're you gonna do?"

Gabe cringed inwardly. "After Cindy died, I buried myself in my work. I've spent the last five years accepting one high profile case after another, and suddenly Emily grows into a young lady. Once she started getting into trouble at school, I knew I had to take a hard look at my life. I realized I had to slow down or lose my daughter too."

Ty leveled his perceptive gaze at his brother. "So you're saying it's time to get back into the game?"

"Actually, there was another woman."

"Were you planning on telling me?"

Gabe shrugged. "I was, until I found out what she really wanted."

"Okay, spill."

"I met this really attractive woman at a Florida Bar Association meeting. We hit it off and started dating, After a couple of weeks, I thought I'd finally let Emily meet her. I wanted to be sure first that she was the type of woman Em would like, that we would all like spending time together.

"Just before I told Em, I found out that this woman had been using me to be noticed by the partners of my firm. With the high-profile cases I'd been working on, she decided to latch on to me and make a name for herself. Needless to say, she wasn't who I thought she was. I really hate it when people lie to me, Ty."

"I know that."

"So, I broke it off and quit dating. Just didn't seem worth it."

"Makes sense, but face it, you can't live your life alone forever. You're only thirty years old. There's plenty of time to go on with your life."

Gabe held up his hand before the on-going debate continued. "Ty—"

"And I know just the woman for you."

Gabe rose from his seat, brushed sawdust off his denim jeans and T-shirt. "Look, I don't need any help."

Ty lifted his eyebrows.

"Or any interference."

"Haven't you noticed that since Em's been hanging out with Dawn Summer, she wants a sister. For that, she needs a mom, a family. Don't tell me you wouldn't like more kids."

"Okay, so maybe I've grudgingly considered getting married again, and I would enjoy more children. The only way that's going to happen is if I start dating again and I told you how I feel about that."

Ty ignored his argument. "I have the perfect candidate?"

Gabe reined in his impatience. "Yeah? Who?"

"Lindsey Summer."

"Lindsey-school-teacher-Summer?"

"Yeah. Got a problem with that?"

His mind flashed back to the scene in his grandmother's parlor. "You know, she came by the house last night." He chuckled. "I had a crush on her in high school. Now she's all grown up. Really grown up."

"You had a thing for her? How come I didn't know about that?"

"I don't know. It was senior year. Ages ago."

"Did you ever go out with her?"

"No. I probably would have asked her to a dance or the movies, but I never got around to it. In fact, near the end of the school year I got an anonymous note asking me to meet this mystery girl at the park in town. I figured it was Lindsey, but when I went to meet her, Cindy was waiting. And the rest . . ."

"Is history."

"Exactly. We started dating, then Lindsey and Cindy had a falling out. Cindy never would tell me what happened, and then, like most things in life, we got busy and forgot about those high school years."

Ty rubbed his chin before speaking his thoughts. "You know, I can really see this. You and Lindsey."

"Ty, don't start. Lindsey's nice and I have fond memories, but I don't know."

"Just give it a try, man. What have you got to lose?"

What did he have to lose? He missed having a woman in his life, but after his last semi-serious relationship, he didn't know if any woman could take Cindy's place.

He glanced at his brother. "Lindsey and I know each other, so there wouldn't be an awkward first date or that getting-to-know-each-other stuff. I guess I could try, but with my hectic life, what do I do if Lindsey starts to get comfortable?"

"Oh, no."

"What?"

"Comfortable? Are you crazy? No woman wants that. I'm telling you, bro, women want sparks. Romance."

"Come to think of it, Lindsey was kind of jumpy any time we were to close to each other last night."

"That's what I'm talking about!"

Realization slowly dawned on Gabe. "Boy, you'd think

I would have caught on. I just thought that since we know each other it wouldn't be a lot of work to start a relationship."

Ty laughed. "There's no such thing. Casey and I worked hard to get our relationship on solid ground, and we still work at it every day. Let me tell you something, love takes work. If it was easy, anyone would have it."

Gabe grinned. "So you're telling me that anything worth having you have to work for?"

"You got it."

"Jeez, Casey's really changed you. I never thought I'd hear this kind of talk coming from my macho, lets-not-reveal-our-feelings big brother."

"Yeah, and if you tell anyone, I'll deny it."

"Your rep is safe with me."

Ty grunted and got up to throw away the lunch trash.

Gabe followed him. "Listen, cut me some slack here. I haven't had to date in a long time."

"So adjust your attitude. Women never want to be known as comfortable."

"Okay, okay, I get the message."

"So when are you gonna get started?"

"Seriously, let me think about this Ty. It's one thing to think about dating in the abstract, quite another to have a flesh-and-blood, good-looking woman like Lindsey to make it feel real. When I'm ready, maybe I'll ask her out to the movies. That's the best I can do right now."

"Sounds like a plan."

Gabe took a deep breath and exhaled. "So, you won't bug me about this anymore?"

"Hey, I forget what we're talking about." Ty grinned wickedly. "But I can't promise that Casey won't."

A loud rendition of Beethoven's Fifth echoed in the empty room. Ty unfastened the cell phone clasped at his belt. "It's got to be Casey. This pregnancy is tough. Do you know how many late-night runs to the store I've made this week alone?"

Gabe grinned. "Enjoy it."

Ty winked. "You bet I will." He pressed the green button. "Hey, darlin'. What's up?"

Gabe walked across the room and picked up the sander, thinking about Emily as a baby. What a great time he'd had as a first-time dad. Nervously taking her home from the hospital, watching as she learned to roll over, then crawl before those first tentative baby steps. Most of all, he loved gazing down in her crib at night as she innocently slumbered, not at all worried with her world when she knew her dad was home. He loved Em so much, couldn't imagine life without her.

Then one day, Em strolled into the kitchen wearing one of Cindy's shirts. Suddenly he realized she wasn't a baby anymore. The older Em got, the more Gabe realized she needed a woman in her life. She was getting to an age where Gabe might not be able to help her out with certain things as a mother could.

Maybe Ty was right. He should take that first step. For Em. Problem was, it was just so darned hard.

Chapter Three

Lindsey squinted as the blow dryer passed by her face once again, wondering yet again how her mother managed to set her up on a date with Ron Silva so quickly.

Laurel Ann pulled and tugged on Lindsey's errant curls for close to 20 minutes now. She started to sweat. How attractive was that for a first date? Finally the infernal dryer went quiet while Laurel Ann stood in front of her, hands on her hips, scrutinizing her styling job.

Lindsey, sitting on the edge of her bed, couldn't read her mother's expression, which made her jumpy. "Well?" she burst out.

Laurel Ann, never one to pass up a chance at drama, circled her daughter before voicing her opinion. "Very nice."

"Just nice?"

"We haven't done your makeup yet. Give me a break here."

Lindsey stood and walked to the mirror above her dresser, ready to give a harsh critique of her hairstyle. She stared at her reflection, eyes wide. "Mom, what did you do?"

"Honey, calm down. It's a bit . . . big, right now, but I have plenty of products to calm it down."

Lindsey sank onto the edge of her bed. "Maybe this isn't such a good idea. I'll probably scare Ron away with this hair."

"Nonsense," her grandmother Dorothea admonished as she came into the room. "Your mama will fix it and the date will be a success."

Lindsey ran her hands through what felt like . . . fuzz.

Laurel Ann hurried out of the bathroom with a tube of one of her hair care products. "Here, we'll just work this in and you'll be surprised at how your hair will lay down."

She squeezed the miracle balm into her hand and began to work it into Lindsey's hair. Lindsey closed her eyes and prayed.

"Besides," Dorothea told them, "Ron's been wanting to date you for a long time. He won't mind a little crazy hair."

"And how do you know this?" Lindsey asked as her mother's movements gave her a headache.

"Everyone knows it."

"Not me."

"That's because you don't pay attention."

Lindsey bit back a retort. No one thought she paid attention to things. She did. But dating hadn't been on her priority list until a few days ago. Before then, men like Ron and Jerry were just nice guys, not potential life mates. And it wasn't that she didn't notice men. She did. It's just that not many seemed to rank up there with Gabe, who ranked very high on her Ideal Man Index.

"Ron is a nice man," her mother added. "He's the general manager at the bank in town. Quite a catch, from what I've heard."

"Then why isn't he married already?"

"I suppose he's picky. Just like you."

Dorothea snorted out a laugh. "That is true, child. You should have been married years ago."

Sage wisdom from two happily married, very dominant females, not afraid to let the world know what they thought. Lindsey was afraid she didn't rate in their league.

She held up her hand. "Point taken. Just fix my hair and let me get this night over with."

"Oh, that's positive." Her mother's sarcasm didn't sit well with Lindsey's less-than-excited mood.

Before an argument could ensue, Dawn strolled into the room. "How's makeover number two going?"

Three different answers bounded in her direction.

"That good? In that case," she turned on her heel, "Granddaddy Ed and I have a serious game of Crazy Eights to finish. Just thought I'd check in."

"Take me with you," Lindsey pleaded, rising from the bed.

"Not a chance," Laurel Ann warned, pushing Lindsey's shoulders back down.

Dawn escaped the room just as Laurel Ann pulled out her suitcase-size cosmetics bag. Lindsey reached up and felt a lock of now-calmed hair loaded down with product. She could tell her hair felt different, but didn't have the courage or the energy to look in the mirror. Better to wait until her mother completely finished the transformation. In the meantime, she could plot how to get rid of these 'helpers' fast so she could redo all of her mother's work before Ron showed up.

Fifteen minutes later, her mother stepped back and sang, "Ta da."

Lindsey sat still, afraid to look in the mirror again.

"You're lovely," Dorothea chimed in.

Slowly, Lindsey rose to get a good look at herself in the mirror. She blinked. Quite a few times. Wide-set eyes with curled lashes stared back at her. And she actually had cheekbones! Her mother had truly done a wonderful job. Lindsey almost didn't recognize herself.

In spite of herself, an errant thought filled her mind. Too bad Gabe couldn't see her like this. Then she quickly squashed the thought. After all, tonight she had a date with Ron. She'd better remember that.

"So?" Laurel Ann prodded.

"I like it, Mom." Lindsey turned to give her mother a hug. "Thanks."

"I just wanted tonight to be special for you."

Lindsey nodded, but wasn't convinced. She was taking this dating strategy slowly. "Okay, everyone leave so I can put on my new outfit. Out. Out."

Laurel Ann made a hasty exit. Dorothea lingered by the door, her usual cheery expression quizzical. "Are you sure you're okay about this dating thing?"

She plastered on a fake smile. Best to keep up appearances with the family while she played along with her sister. "It's what I have to do. At least until Risa moves on to her next crazy notion."

"You don't have to do this."

"It will work out. You know Risa, by next week she'll probably change her mind."

"If you're sure . . ."

Lindsey crossed the room to embrace her grandmother. The voice of reason in her life. "I'm sure."

Dorothea lifted her hand to touch Lindsey's cheek. "You're a dear to do this."

"If it means Dawn stays with us, then I can handle it."

Her grandmother wagged a finger at her. "Just don't let your mother get too carried away here. She's latched onto your sister's ultimatum as an excuse to parade you around town."

She grinned, knowing that Dorothea and her daughter-in-law didn't always see eye to eye. "I know that."

"Well then, I'll let you finish getting ready."

Lindsey watched the door to her room close before casting a critical eye in the mirror again. Okay, the cosmetics really brightened her face. And she had to admit, she liked her hair straighter than normal. All in all, she looked good.

For the wrong man.

Thoughts of Gabe filled her head again, just as they had with amazing frequency since he moved back to town. How on earth could she really give any guy a chance when she mentally compared them to Gabe? And considering the way she felt about Gabe? Oh boy. He made her feel like a carefree teen again, teetering on the verge of a serious schoolgirl crush. None of the single guys in town stood a chance.

Shaking her head, Lindsey went to the closet to remove her new dress, a little red number her mother insisted she buy. When Ron called yesterday, all of her family had been around. With them watching her and trying to listen, she had no choice but to accept his invitation to dinner. Since Dawn's future rested on her shoulders, she'd go along with the dating plan and appease her sister for now. With Risa's penchant for changing her mind, next week she might decide the marriage ultimatum was a mistake. Lindsey blew out a deep breath, hoping for just that.

After donning the red silky dress that did an admirable job of showing off her figure and long legs, she added the finishing touches of gold jewelry and strappy ruby sandals. Her dark hair shined in the light as she ran the brush through one last time. A final spritz of Glow and she was ready.

When she entered the living room, all eyes went to her.

Laurel Ann beamed, Gramma nodded, Dawn grinned and Granddaddy Ed frowned.

She dropped some tissues in her purse and stopped. "What?"

Dawn stared at her with wide eyes. "You look great."

Everyone started talking at once.

Lindsey held her hand up. "Whoa." She stood before the lone male in the room. "Do I get your approval, Granddaddy?" she asked as she twirled around.

"Just let me get my shotgun so the boy knows not to mess with my granddaughter."

Lindsey laughed and placed a kiss on the older man's leathery cheek. "Remember, we don't want to scare him away."

"I'm just sayin' . . .", her grandfather muttered.

"Besides," Dorothea added, "Ed can't see distance without his glasses, which he refuses to wear, so he isn't getting anywhere near his shotgun. He couldn't hit the side of a barn," she whispered to Lindsey.

"My eyes may be bad, but my hearin' works fine."

Dawn played her last heart card with a flourish while Ed muttered about losing again. "Papa said he'd take me to the library if Mr. Banner can't give us a ride. Is that okay?"

Lindsey's heart nearly stopped beating. "Mr. Banner? Coming here to pick you up?"

"I don't know. Em hasn't called yet."

Just great. That's all Lindsey needed. Gabe showing up on her doorstep at the same time as Ron. Looks like she might get her wish after all, Gabe catching her all decked out.

Dorothea changed the subject. "So where is your date taking you tonight?"

"We're having dinner at the Magnolia Inn."

"It's a lovely place." Dorothea's tone took on a wistful air. "Your grandfather took me there once."

"And it cost a fortune."

"Oh, Ed. Where's your sense of romance?"

"We've been married nearly fifty years. That says romance."

Lindsey chuckled at Granddaddy. He might fuss and protest, but by the glimmer in Ed's eyes, he still deeply loved Gramma.

"I promise to fill you in when I get home," she told her grandmother. Glancing at her watch, she took a deep breath. "Ron should be here any minute."

As if on cue, the doorbell rang. Dawn bolted out of her chair to answer the door.

Lindsey adjusted her bracelet, thinking it was most likely Ron. Until she heard Emily's chattering voice followed by the lower timbre of a man. Gabe, to be precise.

She ran back to the bedroom, checked her Coral Craving lipstick, then sauntered out, casually acting like Gabe always stopped by unannounced when she had a date. "Gabe, how nice to see you again."

Gabe looked up from watching the girls. The smile on his face froze for seconds before he spoke. "Sorry, is this a bad time to stop by? We were around the corner . . ."

"Nope," Dawn piped in.

Gabe's gaze fell to Lindsey's silky dress, then back to her face. "You look real nice, Lindsey. Real nice."

"Doesn't she though?" Dorothea gushed. "She has a date."

"Who better not keep her out late," Ed mumbled.

"And she's so excited," Laurel Ann finished.

Lindsey felt her cheeks grow warm, figuring they must match the same shade of red as her dress.

Gabe slipped his hands in the front pockets of his jeans, calling attention to his long legs. Just as the other night she'd seen him, he was dressed casually, but instead of a chest hugging T-shirt, he wore a white golf shirt that showed off his naturally tanned skin. "In that case, please don't let us take up your time. C'mon, girls, let's go."

The girls blew kisses to the room in general and skipped out the door. Lindsey could hear Em's voice as she followed the pair heading down the porch stairs to the car. "Too bad your mom isn't going out with my dad tonight."

Lindsey stopped on the top step and grimaced, hoping Gabe had missed that.

He hadn't, by the matching grimace on his face, although Lindsey thought he tried admirably to hide his amused expression.

Gabe slowly followed the girls, but not before he glanced back at Lindsey one last time. "Have a nice evening."

"Thanks."

As soon as the girls closed the car door, Lindsey felt a heavy weight settle in her stomach. She hurried down the steps in time to catch Gabe before he got into the sleek, silver Lexus. "Gabe, wait."

He stopped, his shuttered gaze traveling over her outfit again, down to her shoes, and back to her face.

"I didn't mean to rush you off. I guess I'm a little nervous. It's a first date."

"Yeah, first dates are like that. Expecting the sparks and all that." He tilted his head. "You really do look great."

"Thanks." She knew her face was coloring again as her stomach did flip-flops at the now obvious flare of interest she glimpsed in his eyes. Why, oh why, couldn't she be slipping into the Lexus tonight, headed out for a nerve-tingling, pulse-pumping date with Gabe? Talk about sparks.

"Who's the lucky guy?"

"Huh? Oh, Ron Silva."

"Ron." He closed his eyes as if trying to picture the man's face. "Was he in school with us?"

"Yes, but a few grades ahead."

He opened his eyes. "Okay, I think I remember. He was president of the Future Businessmen Club." His lips quirked upward. "So, where are you going?"

"The Magnolia Inn."

"Nice place."

"So I've heard. I'll find out shortly."

"Make sure you order the chocolate turtle pie for dessert."

She nodded. "Thanks for mentioning it."

They stood in the evening shadows with the moon just beginning to show. The first blossoms of spring scented the night air. What a perfect night, standing here with Gabe.

While she waited for another man.

"I'll see you," he said, then opened the door and slid into the driver's seat.

Lindsey stood and watched the tail lights disappear, wishing she was going with them.

"You know," Laurel Ann said from the porch, "he isn't dating. Best to keep that in mind."

Lindsey wistfully sighed. "You don't have to remind me." That said, she climbed the steps to wait for her date.

"Your dad was awful quiet on the way over here," Dawn said as the girls dropped a pile of books on the empty table in the far corner of the library building. They loved to meet here, away from the prying eyes of most adults. In their corner, the girls could read to their hearts' content and dream about the future.

"I know. I think he was surprised to see your mom all dressed up. She looked so pretty."

"Do you think he wants to ask her out?"

Em shrugged. "I've never seen him look at any other woman like that. And believe me, I've tried to get him to notice."

"You know they went to school together."

"Dad said so when I came home from school the first day and I told him who my teacher was. He smiled kinda funny, like adults do when they remember things."

Dawn stared down at the cover of *Little Women.* "Maybe we could try harder to get them to like each other." Her eyes lit up. "Oh, I wish they'd get married." She paused for a moment before speaking her deepest, secret thought. "Then we could really be sisters."

Em scooted to the edge of her chair. "We could be a real family."

Dawn bit her bottom lip, afraid to really wish for the dream buried in her heart. "So, what's the plan?"

"I know. I'll get Gran to help us. She's the best matchmaker I know. She married off Aunt Marilyn to Dusty."

"And my Granddaddy Ed would help, I just know he would," Dawn added.

Em fished in her backpack and pulled out paper and a pencil. "First thing we have to do is think of ways we can get them together."

"Okay, that's good. Oh, they just have to fall in love. Just like in *Little Women.*" She tapped the cover of the book then looked down at the paper. "What do we have so far?"

"Nothing," Em complained. Suddenly an impish glint came into her eyes. "I've got it! We'll get them together, starting tonight."

"How? She's on a date with Ron."

"With my idea, that date won't stand a chance."

Chapter Four

T*his date didn't stand a chance.*

Lindsey glanced around the elegantly appointed room of the Magnolia Inn for what seemed like the hundredth time. Ron talked to the owner while she admired the southern charm of the room. Built in the 1800s, the house had been family owned for generations. Muted lighting cast romantic shadows over the diners. The walls were papered in a satin covering. Heavy velvet drapes flanked the long windows. Aged woodwork graced the molding and floor while lovely impressionist paintings like Monet hung on the walls. And the delicious aroma of freshly baked rolls came from the direction of the kitchen, making her stomach growl.

"Don't you think we should order?" Lindsey cut in on Ron's running dialogue about . . . himself.

"Certainly. Would you allow me to do the honors?"

Great. A self-appointed gentleman. She feared he'd probably order the worse entree on the menu. "Thanks, but how about a recommendation?" she asked, hoping to put in her own vote for the meal.

"The Boeuf Bourguignonne is wonderful. I've had that myself. Of course, the fresh salmon is quite tasty."

"I couldn't help but notice the rosemary chicken. I'll bet it's wonderful too."

Ron's eyebrow's angled as he thought. "I've never tried the chicken." He closed the menu. "I've come to a decision."

Lindsey smiled to herself as Ron placed his order with the waitress. She may not be enjoying the best date in recorded history, but at least she'd get something she liked to eat. Taking a sip of her water, she viewed Ron over the rim of her glass. He was good looking, in an aloof sort of way. Which really cracked her up, since she knew him wearing thick lens glasses and braces when he grew up on a small farm not too far out of town. He spoke of how he'd done well as the general manager of the Paineville Savings and Loan, and in his quest for the good life, had climbed the social ladder, which seemed very important to him. He went on and on about his job, his business interests and his life. Now she recalled why she never dated him before.

"You should come to an investment club meeting. We have a speaker every month. It's really fascinating."

"I'm sure it is, but since I'm on the library board, I've been busy. The gala fundraiser is next month, and I have to get ready for the literacy program I'm presenting to the governor."

"Your mother told me about the gala. It will be quite a night."

Lindsey hastily swallowed her water, nearly choking in the process. What on earth had possessed her mother to mention the gala to Ron? She crossed her fingers under the table, hoping her mother hadn't cajoled him into asking to be her escort. "For everyone else it will be fun. For me, it'll be work. I'll be busy, busy, busy."

"All work and no play?"

"Yes. I'm planning and coordinating the entire affair." *With a committee,* she admitted silently, but he didn't have to know that. "And getting ready for the literacy program has taken up a big bulk of my time."

He held out his glass in salute. "Then I should be honored that you could have dinner with me tonight."

Their dinner arrived and the conversation moved from investments and literacy programs, to national news and local gossip. Ron proved to be very well read and knowledgeable about things, but where was the spark? The bit of magic? The delicious sense of romance in the air?

It would have to come in the form of dessert.

"The turtle pie is supposed to be excellent," she said.

"Two, please," Ron told the waiter. "Since you haven't dined here, who informed you about the pie?"

"Um, Gabe Banner."

"Ah, yes, Banner. Heard he had moved back to town."

"With his daughter. They're living with Ruby Sue."

Ron laughed. "That woman drives me crazy. Always bringing in her bank statement to complain about the charges and demanding a senior discount. We're a bank, for Pete's sake. We don't give discounts." He looked at Lindsey, realizing he'd wandered off the topic. "Didn't you used to hang around with Gabe?"

"A little bit, but more with his wife, Cindy. We were best friends once."

"Tragic loss."

Lindsey frowned. "Yes. It was."

As much as she knew Cindy's death devastated Gabe and Emily, she had also grieved for her old friend when she'd heard the news, despite how they'd ended things.

Once Gabe and Cindy had started dating, Lindsey had kept her distance. Had to really, since she wouldn't be much of a friend pining over Cindy's boyfriend. Their friendship became strained after the note incident, but in her heart she'd always had fond memories of their childhood.

"—suppose he'll remarry," Ron was saying as she surfaced from her thoughts.

"Excuse me?"

"Gabe. Remarrying? I commented that I'd heard he hasn't made any steps to remarry."

Lindsey tried to control the beating of her heart at the words Gabe and remarry. "I suppose in time."

The desserts arrived just as a commotion in the foyer caught Lindsey's attention. She leaned out of her chair to see what was happening just as Dawn and Emily burst into the entrance foyer.

"What on earth?" She removed her napkin from her lap and stood. "Excuse me for a minute."

She made her way through the room to see the owner hushing the girls and checking to make sure they were all right.

"Mom!" Dawn hurried over.

"What are you girls doing here?"

The girls spoke over each other in their haste to explain. Lindsey held up one hand until they stopped talking, then pointed to Dawn.

"Mr. Banner didn't pick us up," she explained, "and we were getting worried. I knew you were having dinner here so we came over."

"I know Dad said he'd pick us up at seven o'clock," Emily piped in.

"And he said in the parking lot, but he wasn't there."

Lindsey looked at her watch: 7:55.

"Maybe you got the time wrong?"

"No, I'm sure that's what he said."

Lindsey looked over at the owner. "Luca, can I use the phone?" she asked, already reaching for the receiver.

"Yes of course," Luca smiled nervously, poking his head into the dining room to be sure his guests weren't disturbed.

"Emily, tell me your home number."

As Emily recited the number, Lindsey pressed the buttons, then waited as the phone rang and rang and rang. "No answer."

"What should we do?" Dawn asked, eyes wide.

"Does he have a cell phone?"

"No, he's been meaning to get one since we moved here, but hasn't gotten around to it."

Lindsey's concern grew. How could Gabe forget the girls? She hoped nothing was wrong. "Let me get my wrap and I'll walk with you back to the library. Maybe this was a misunderstanding." She went back into the dining room, explained the situation to Ron and begged his forgiveness, but she had to leave. The girls were standing by the door when she returned. "Let's go."

The cool night air grazed Lindsey's skin, giving her the chills. She pulled the black pashmina shawl tighter around her as she tried to keep up with the girls who hurried along with sneakers on their feet while she tried to make tracks in high heels.

They reached the walkway to the library just as Gabe pushed out of the doors and raced down the steps. His eyes widened in surprise when he spied Lindsey.

"Lindsey?" His gaze ran over her as if seeing her for the very first time tonight, then slowly his look heated as he viewed her dress again. She remembered the excitement she'd felt earlier from that stare, only this time it multiplied. No way was she going to quell the pleasure that bubbled up inside her at his fixed attention by saying a word to break this spell.

Then Gabe looked at the girls as if noticing them for the first time. "What happened? I thought I told you girls to wait by the front doors?"

"We did, Dad, but you weren't here. So we went to get Miss Summer."

"But she was on a date."

"She didn't look like she was having much fun," Emily reasoned.

Gabe glanced in Lindsey's direction, his dark gaze burning hers for a fleeting moment. Then his expression softened to concern when he spoke to her. "I'm sorry about this."

He touched her shoulder to emphasize his sincerity, sending waves of desire over her body. As much as she wanted this moment to continue, they had a situation here. She'd deal with the girls before dealing with her out-of-control reaction to Gabe.

"Did you give the girls instructions about where to meet them?"

"Implicit instructions. I told them to wait out by the front doors at seven-thirty. They were nowhere to be found."

"Girls, you said seven in the parking lot."

"Oops." Emily grinned and shrugged.

Dawn lowered her eyes. "I guess we made a mistake."

Lindsey crossed her arms over her chest. She smelled a rat. Well, two rats, actually. "Somehow they conveniently managed to misunderstand you."

Gabe put on his best fatherly frown and leveled the girls with his stare. "I was worried about you two. Promise you won't go off again like that or I'll restrict your library time, Emily."

"Okay, Dad."

Gabe glanced up at Lindsey, noticing the way she tugged the shawl around her shoulders and tried to hide the amusement lingering in her eyes. Her lips pursed in a reluctant smile.

"Why don't you girls go wait for me in the car."

The girls gave each other a knowing glance, smiled triumphantly, then headed in the direction of the parking lot.

"I'm sorry about this. Em is usually so dependable. I don't know what's gotten into her lately."

Lindsey pulled her shawl tighter. "No damage was done. They meant well."

Gabe brushed his hand through his hair. "Who am I kidding? This has been Emily's usual modus operandi. She was good here for a while, I thought maybe she was settling down."

"It really could have been an honest mistake," Lindsey offered out of politeness.

Gabe looked at the Lexus, a remnant from his law days, to make sure the girls were there, then back to Lindsey. She also looked in the direction of the girls, with a contemplative look on her face.

"What's wrong?"

"Hmm?" She shook her head just a tiny bit. "I was just thinking."

"About what?"

Her lips curved into a rueful smile. "I didn't know what to think when the girls showed up at the Inn. I thought either you were in trouble or you just plain forgot them."

He chuckled. "Thanks for hearing me out before reaching the wrong conclusion."

"Thank my years of experience as a teacher. I've learned to keep my opinions to myself until I've heard the entire story."

"Good approach, especially with kids."

She smiled again, and he couldn't help but notice, for the second time tonight, how dynamite she looked. Her hair was beginning to curl just a bit at the ends and he wouldn't be surprised if her unruly curls returned, just like he remembered her during high school.

And her dress, well, he didn't want to go there. He hadn't stopped admiring women since Cindy died, but until Lindsey, he hadn't realized that a soft, feminine outfit could take his breath away. And Lindsey had done just that. Taken his breath away.

Only she had a date with another guy.

"I'm sorry the girls intruded on your date. Can I give you a ride back to the Inn?"

She waved off his offer. "To be truthful, the evening ended long before the girls showed up. Ron Silva's a nice guy, but not for me."

Gabe's mood brightened. He tried hard not to sound pleased. "So, then, the girls did you a favor?"

"I suppose they did."

A taut moment passed as Gabe tried to think of something to say. A beat-up truck lumbered by, making enough racket to wake the dead. Lindsey shifted, lifting her foot to rub the sides of her shoe.

"Are you okay?"

"Sure. Just not used to sprinting down the block in high heels."

"Look, why don't I give you a ride home. I'm taking Dawn anyway, and since you no longer have a date . . ."

"I accept. And quickly, before these shoes squeeze my feet numb."

He held out his arm, hesitating just a fraction at the surprise reflected in Lindsey's eyes. She obliged and draped long tapered fingers over his arm. At the initial touch she steadied herself, then visibly let out a breath and walked in time with him as he led her to the car.

"I was thinking maybe we could get coffee and some dessert at the Pastry Palace, but I don't suppose we should encourage the girls' behavior by taking them with us."

"Hey, they made me miss my dessert. I'm all for your idea."

Lindsey's smile gave Gabe a kick to the gut. He found himself wanting to make her smile every time he was in her company. Her green eyes lit up and a cute dimple formed in her cheek.

"If this was a usual thing with them, then I might worry," she added. "It's Friday night, there's no school tomorrow, so why not live dangerously. I guess we can let them come."

He grinned. "I like your attitude."

All too quickly they reached the car and Gabe reluctantly released her arm to open the passenger door. Lindsey slid in, giving him a glimpse of attractive legs where the hem of her dress rode up just a little.

He jogged around the front of the car and opened his door. "Okay," he told the girls as he angled in. "We took a vote and decided to let this misunderstanding go for now." He half-turned in the seat and frowned at them. "Let's not make this a habit."

Both girls, wide-eyed, nodded. He didn't buy the innocent act for a minute. He winked at Lindsey as he started the ignition.

Within minutes they pulled up to the Pastry Palace. The girls tumbled out of the car and ran inside. Gabe met Lindsey as she exited the car, once again adjusting her shawl.

"Here," he said, slipping off his denim jacket. "Put this on. You look cold."

Again, she hesitated, then accepted his jacket. A funny shiver went through him when she draped the jacket, still warm with his body heat, over her shoulders. He mentally shook his head, not wanting to analyze his reaction right this moment.

Once inside, Gabe ordered coffee and the girls talked him into a Double Doozy—a double cream-stuffed chocolate cookie sandwich with enough sugar to keep them wired for hours.

"You're going to regret this," Lindsey scolded as she watched the girls dig into their treats.

"I figure the sugar-shock will hit Em in about an hour and she'll sleep it off."

"Spoken like an indulgent father."

"Do you think that? That I'm indulgent?"

Lindsey reached over and touched his hand. Her soft skin left a tingling trail across his hand. "I was just kidding. I know it's hard as a single parent. I see the effect a one-parent household can have on some of my students, and believe me, Em is great. She's respectful, does her work and is a leader among the children."

"Maybe a little too much. She seems to be leading Dawn down her slippery slope."

"Her sometime lack of, shall I say focus, is easy to take into consideration when weighed against the other traits. You've done a beautiful job, Gabe. I mean it, not just because I'm her teacher. Or your friend."

Pride swelled in his chest and he found it hard to speak.

"Cindy would be proud of both of you."

He nodded, knowing his late wife would be pleased.

Lindsey sipped her coffee, then asked, "How are you settling in now that you're back in town?"

"Can't complain. Em's taken to school, thanks to you, no doubt, Gran makes us earn our keep, and Ty put me straight to work once I finished up my outstanding law cases."

"So you're really not going to practice law?"

"Looks that way."

"So, if someone needed some legal advice, say, for a friend, have you got any recommendations on who to see?"

He chose not to query her private life, just in case she was asking for herself. "I refer folks to Tom Lyndon in town. He handles family law. Seems to have a good rep too."

"I'm familiar with Tom."

Now that got his attention. "Really? In a professional capacity?"

Her eyebrows raised. "A girl can't give away all her secrets, Mr. Banner."

"And she has a big one," Dawn chimed in through a mouthful of cookie.

Lindsey gaped at her niece, piquing Gabe's interest.

"Care to tell all?"

"I can't. You're not my lawyer, so there's no client/attorney privileges."

He duly noted the playful teasing in her voice. "And Tom will get to have those privileges?"

"You could say that."

The thought of Tom and Lindsey sharing secrets bothered Gabe. It shouldn't, he knew. Could it be a twinge of jealousy? No, he rationalized. Not that.

He'd just come back to town and there were years since Lindsey and he had been friends. Even though he'd been attracted to her in high school, he really didn't know what turn her life had taken since then. Or her personal interests. Who was he to pry where he might not be wanted? Just because he entertained thoughts of dating her didn't give him the right to stick his nose in her affairs.

No matter how much he wanted to.

"Well, I'm sure Tom will be a good lawyer for you."

"And he's not married," Dawn added.

Lindsey's eyes widened. "How on earth do you know that?"

"Grammy told me. The other day we were sitting at the kitchen table and I was playing with her makeup kit. She was making a list of eligible men for you to marry."

Gabe watched Lindsey's face turn pale.

"I could see some of the names, until she covered it over when she caught me reading it."

Emily regarded Dawn seriously. "She must have a plan too."

Dawn nodded. "But I don't think it's as good as ours."

Gabe, sensing Lindsey's shock at the news, decided to stop the conversation. "That's enough, girls. Why don't you go to the restroom and clean the cookie crumbs from your mouth."

The girls reluctantly left the adults, chattering about plans as they crossed the room.

"Your grammy has a head start on us," Emily mumbled.

"But we ruined the first date, so it doesn't count," Dawn quickly countered as they pushed open the door to the restroom and disappeared inside.

Gabe turned his questioning gaze on her. "Why would your mother make a list of men for you?"

She groaned. "It's a long story."

"Look, Lindsey, I know it's been a long time since we've seen each other, but with your questions about lawyers and your mom's list . . . is everything alright?"

"Well . . ."

"Please, tell me. Maybe I can help. Anything at all, just name it. What do you need?"

"I need a husband."

Chapter Five

"Want to run that by me again?"

Oh no, did I just blurt that out? Lindsey wanted to bury her burning face in her hands, but the damage was done. Instead, she looked Gabe right in the eye.

"You heard right. My sister won't give me full, legal custody of Dawn unless I get married." Not that it was a secret, at least to the members of her family. But she hadn't meant to say anything to Gabe. He must think her a total airhead. Or a desperate spinster.

At his surprised look, she continued. "I'm sorry, that sounded really bad." She filled him in on Risa's shaky past, the failed marriage and birth of a daughter she couldn't take care of. Lindsey's voice filled with emotion when she told him how she'd raised Dawn as her own. "My sister blows into town, tells me she wants me to get married so I can keep Dawn, then leaves, knowing I'll take care of the problem."

"So that explains Dawn's remarks."

"Yes. I've decided to play along, make it look like I'm

seriously dating to give Risa time to change her mind. She usually does."

"Maybe Risa has other intentions. Maybe she plans on settling down?"

Lindsey shook her head. "Not likely. As I said, she doesn't do the domestic scene. Even though Dawn is older and, therefore, easier to drag around, I'd like to think that deep down, Risa has enough sense to see that wouldn't be good for an eleven year old."

"What does Dawn think?"

"I've tried keeping as much from her as possible, I mean, Risa may come up with wacky ideas and she may not be terribly responsible, but she is Dawn's mother and I don't want my niece thinking badly of her. She understands that her mother will never bake cookies with her or tuck her into bed at night, but the fact that Risa shows up from time to time gives her a connection of sorts. Dawn needs stability and she gets it from my family and it needs to stay that way."

"So that's why you've been in contact with Tom Lyndon."

"Well, kind of. I've talked to him a few times, but the family had decided not to do anything from a legal standpoint. But with my sister's latest demand, I need plenty of advice."

He seemed to think about that for a while. "Therefore, the need for a husband."

"Exactly."

"And you're okay with that?"

"Of course not. It sounds so . . . mercenary. But I love Dawn too much to lose her, so I've decided to play along until Risa comes to her senses."

She stared down into her now empty coffee cup and thought about her love for children and her inability to have any. "I think it would kill me more than Dawn if Risa took her away."

And those words were true. She couldn't love Dawn any more than if she'd given birth to the girl herself. The bond had been there from the beginning, from the first time Lindsey held out her finger and Dawn's tiny hand grasped hold like it was a lifeline. With pride, Lindsey had watched Dawn take her first steps and say her first words. She held back tears on Dawn's first day in kindergarten and beamed with love when Dawn sang like an angel in her first solo with the children's church choir.

Still, she prayed that she'd find the right man. A man who'd make a good husband as well as a devoted father.

Gabe's question broke off her thoughts. "So your mother is making a list of eligible bachelors?"

She rolled her eyes. "It's news to me, but it appears so. I can't believe Dawn knows. My mother and I *will* be having a discussion when I see her."

"Sounds like she's taking the dating scenario seriously."

"Too seriously, it you ask me."

"Getting married is a serious proposition."

"Oh, I don't really think it'll go that far." She didn't like being put on the spot by Risa. She understood that her sister had deep-seated issues, and for so many years Lindsey had worked with her, just to keep Dawn at home. Now she'd upped the ante and put Lindsey in an unenviable position.

Lindsey glanced at Gabe as he seemed to ponder her situation. She couldn't believe she was actually sitting here with him, carrying on this conversation.

"Sounds like you've got your work cut out for you, Linds."

Lindsey fought back a shiver when she heard Gabe call her by her old nickname. His husky, teasing voice, calling her by that name, suggested an intimacy that wasn't there, even though she had felt the mutual stirring of attraction between them tonight. She shook off her wishes. "Gosh, it's been so many years since anyone called me that."

Gabe grinned. "We had fun as kids. You and Cindy were great friends."

True, they were, until the day Lindsey confided in Cindy about the note Lindsey had sent to Gabe, asking him to meet her at a designated bench in the park. It had taken every ounce of confidence within her to even write the note, then carry out the plan. Finding her best friend waiting in her place for the guy she had a wicked crush on, then see them become a couple, had strained their friendship. Gabe never knew that Lindsey had written the note, so if he noticed the tension between the girls, he never said a word. And she didn't think Cindy ever told him who really sent the note. If the tables had been turned, and she'd been devious enough to show up in Cindy's place, she never would have mentioned that fact to Gabe. She still thought it best to keep the truth to herself.

"I always thought it was too bad we lost touch," Gabe continued, unaware of her unwelcome stroll down memory lane.

"Well, you moved to Florida and I went to teacher's college, so I suppose it's natural to get busy and lose track of friends."

"Before Cindy died she talked about coming up here to visit, but we never got around to it. She would have liked seeing you again. She never said what happened to cause the fallout between you two, but she was sorry and always regretted it."

Lindsey clamped her mouth shut, hoping Gabe would let it go and not ask for details. She certainly never would have wished any calamity on Cindy, and in retrospect, maybe they could have hashed out the past and come to some sort of friendship.

"It's over now. Can't change the past, you know."

"My thoughts exactly." Gabe grinned at her, and before she could change the topic, the girls returned from the restroom. Gabe loaded them up and drove them back to the cottage. Em stayed in the car while he walked Lindsey and Dawn to the front door.

"Thank you for the ride and the cookie," Dawn said as she pointedly glanced between the two of them. "I'm going in now."

"Goodnight, Dawn."

"I'll be right in." Lindsey turned on the top step, coming eye to eye with Gabe, close enough to lean forward for a goodnight kiss. Another stab of longing pierced her heart, but she pushed it away, thankful that her voice sounded normal when she spoke. "Thanks, Gabe. It's been an . . . interesting night."

"Listen, if you have any legal questions, I'm sure I could help you out."

She heard the politeness in his voice, but not the conviction. "Tom will do just fine," she said, seeing the obvious relief play across his face. "Besides, you're not practicing anymore, remember?"

"Yeah."

"I hate to tell you this, but you're not very good at this quitting thing."

"Right. Thanks."

"Anytime."

Reluctantly, she slipped off Gabe's jacket, memorizing the softness of the worn denim, the tantalizing scent of Drakkar that clung to the fabric, and now bathed her skin. She handed the garment back to him, again experiencing tremors of pleasure as her hand grazed his in the exchange. He smiled up at her and her toes curled. Nobody had a smile like his. Nobody.

"I guess I should call it a night," she said, trying for levity in the light of all the things she'd shared with Gabe tonight.

Holding back a sigh, she reached for the doorknob, ready to go inside.

"Maybe I can help with the dating thing?"

His statement stopped her cold. She blinked at him just to be sure she heard him right. Her heart skipped a beat. "Excuse me?"

"I might know a single guy or two to add to the list."

A wave of disappointment washed over her and she tried to keep her voice light when she spoke. "Thanks, but Mom has that covered."

"That's right. With her list."

Lindsey laughed. "Apparently my mother is filling my social agenda quickly. And with the literacy gala coming up, it'll just be one party after another. I'm turning into a regular party girl."

Gabe's smiled waned and he took a step back. His body language definitely showed that something bothered him. Was it her joking about her social life?

She glanced at him one final time before opening the door. "Goodnight, Gabe."

" 'Night, Linds."

A regular party girl. He didn't need to hear that.

As he drove through the dark night, his thoughts focused on Lindsey. Her parting words really bothered him. Especially when he couldn't quite picture Lindsey with a party-girl image. Of course, he hadn't kept up with Lindsey in years. Maybe that lifestyle came natural to her?

He frowned, glancing in the rearview mirror to see Emily. He grinned. Just as he thought, the sugar high had crashed and his daughter had fallen sound asleep.

Leaving him with his own counsel as he debated the issue of party-girl Lindsey in his mind. No, she cared too much about her niece to be involved with a party crowd. That much came out loud and clear when he talked to her. She loved her job working with children. She still lived near her parents.

Still . . . he found his renewed attraction to her unsettling. The night she'd come to Gran's house, he figured her allure was the pleasure of seeing an old friend again after so many years. But after seeing her tonight, in that hot red dress, he realized his response to her was purely male. Totally male. Oh, yeah, he wanted to see her again. And not as just a friend.

Then he thought of his lame offer to help find her a date and groaned out loud. What was he thinking? He should have asked her out for himself. Lindsey was both beautiful and intelligent, a heady combination. But did he want to get involved with her, in light of her family problems? Did he dare let Emily dream of having a family when he couldn't promise a happily ever after? He thought and thought, then let out a strained laugh.

It was already too late.

"So where is this list I've heard about?" Lindsey marched into her mother's kitchen the next morning, ready to do battle.

Laurel Ann, already in full makeup so early in the morning, sipped from a mug of coffee. The slight smile playing around her lips gave her away. "What list?"

"Don't pull that innocent act on me. You know what list.

The one featuring eligible bachelors in the greater Paine-ville area as potential dates."

"Paineville? Honey, my list travels all the way to the Mason-Dixon line."

Lindsey gaped at her mother. "Please don't tell me you're serious."

"Oh, but I am."

Lindsey groaned. "That's what I was afraid of."

"It's not like this is the end of the world. You'll meet some interesting men in the process. How many women can say they have so many men to choose from?"

"Okay, I don't want to seem ungrateful here, but just how many men are you lining up for me?"

"Just a handful."

"Please be more specific."

"I've only called the top five. So far I'm waiting to see how they work out before contacting the others." ˙

"Mom, you can't do this. It's crazy. Not to mention scary. And it's just not me."

"Well that's the point. If you had your way, you'd never go out, but keep pining away for Gabe Banner."

Lindsey swallowed the lump that insisted on working its way up her throat. Apparently, he wasn't looking. He'd made that pretty clear last night with his parting comments.

"I know that, Mom. I also know that I'm not going to go out with a bunch of guys, then narrow the field down to one man because of a deadline. This isn't a TV reality show here, this is my life."

"And Dawn's."

Lindsey took a deep breath, sat down, and rested her elbows on the kitchen table.

"Coffee? I just brewed it."

"Thanks." Lindsey silently stewed for a full minute as her mother poured her a mug and handed it to her. "I can't believe Risa would do this. And now she's got the whole family in on the act."

Laurel Ann took a seat opposite Lindsey at the table.

"I really blame myself, you know. If your father and I had been better parents when she was young, maybe she would have turned out more like you. But we were kids ourselves."

"I still don't know how you and dad did it."

Laurel Ann smiled dreamily. "It had to be love."

Lindsey silently envied her parents' relationship. Imagine, high school sweethearts finding their soul mate at such a young age. Lindsey sighed and rested her elbow on the table, dropping her chin in her palm. Of course, things hadn't always gone smoothly.

Laurel Ann had wanted to leave the Georgia mountains and break into modeling. William, on the other hand, did not want to go. He'd started a farm equipment repair business and needed to stick around so it would grow. In the meantime, Laurel Ann sent photos out to different companies, but never heard anything and soon the couple had gotten married. A year later, she sent out a second round of photos and within months, she received the call and signed a contract. She agreed to move to Los Angeles, and William reluctantly agreed. So they took baby Risa and headed out to California.

As much as Lindsey loved the mountains here, her mother's resolve to pack up her family and move out west so she could pursue her dream of a modeling career still affected her. It showed Lindsey that if you put your mind to a dream, anything could happen.

For many years Laurel Ann was successful. They lived in LA and built their family, which now included Lindsey. Laurel Ann began dragging Risa to her many shoots when the young girl showed an interest in her mother's work.

Risa was the darling, and lived life for the spoiling that came with that title. As a result, she became more than a bit wild. By the time Lindsey was five, her father decided to return to Georgia, taking her with him. Risa stayed with Laurel Ann. From then on, Lindsey and her dad spent half the year in Georgia where he could tend to his business, and the other half in LA while a trusted hired hand filled in when he was gone.

Lindsey remembered how she loved to look at the pictures her mother let her take from her modeling portfolio. Even though her father always said he was thrilled to be back in the mountains, he still beamed with pride at his wife's success. Lindsey was too young to understand why her father wanted to go home without her mother, but she still admired the strength of their marriage to survive living apart for many years.

When Laurel Ann reached her mid-30s, the demand for her famous face on magazines waned. Never one to depend on one sure thing, she had developed a working relationship with a skin care company and they offered her the position of spokesperson. She eventually bought the company, naming it Laurel Ann Skinmetics and returned home, moving the company with her. The family reunited, but Risa hated living the rural life. It made her miserable, thus everyone else was miserable. And then she left town.

"Why on earth do we let her run us around like she does?" Lindsey asked, frustrated.

"For Dawn. But unfortunately, it means we contribute to Risa's problem. She knows we'll take care of Dawn no matter what, because we adore her."

So for Dawn, they would all walk through the fire.

Or go on a cockamamie husband hunt to appease her.

"I happened to notice that Gabe brought you home last

night," Laurel Ann commented much too neutrally, which meant she was really peeved.

"It's a long story."

"I want to hear everything."

"Okay." Lindsey took a sip of her coffee while deciding where to begin. "Look, Mom, I know you think Ron was a good choice, but we didn't . . . connect. I don't know how to explain it. There was no interest, no spark."

Her mother let out a longsuffering sigh. "Darn. I was really hoping that would work out."

"Well, you tried."

Laurel Ann tapped her crimson fingernails against her cheek. "How could I have been so off about him. Hmm. I might have to rework the list."

"Mom, let's not get carried away here."

"So how did you end up with Gabe, even though I don't think I want to know the answer to that question."

"When Gabe wasn't at the library to pick up Dawn and Emily, they became worried. Dawn remembered that I'd be at the Inn, so they came to get me. Turns out they got the time wrong, because Gabe was looking for them while they were with me. Anyway, Ron and I called it a night and we took the girls for a treat and Gabe drove us home. End of story."

End of story, for sure, after Gabe's backpedaling when they said goodnight.

Lindsey glanced all around the room, not wanting to meet her mother's eyes. She wished she could figure out why his demeanor had changed.

"That's it?"

"Yep."

"Then why don't I believe you?"

Lindsey gave in and looked at her mom. "What's not to believe?"

"Honey, every time you mention that man's name you get all la-la. How on earth will you ever find a man if you keep thinking about Gabe?" She stood and carried her mug to the sink. "I just don't think that meeting was coincidental."

"Mom, how could it be otherwise?"

Laurel Ann tapped the table, her acrylic nails sounding out the beat. She squinted her eyes in a determination to get to the bottom of this. "I don't know, but I'll figure it out."

Lindsey rose. "You do that. And while that burning question keeps you busy, I have some papers to correct." She headed for the back door. Lately, living so close to her family members was making her crazy with all this matchmaking nonsense. What she wouldn't give right now, to live in her own house, on her own property—maybe in Siberia? This wasn't the first time she'd had this thought.

In her mind flashed the image of the Olsen house located downtown, a few blocks off the town square. Lindsey's perfect dream house.

She sighed. Another dream that had to take a back seat to reality.

"Do you know where Dawn is?" she checked with her mother before leaving.

"With Ed. I saw them headed to the barn with Emily in tow."

"Em's here?"

"You see? You don't even know if Gabe dropped her by and you get all giddy, for heaven's sake."

Lindsey blew out a frustrated breath and walked out to the porch. As she headed for the cottage, a tiny smile played on her lips. If Em was here, Gabe couldn't be too far behind.

Chapter Six

"Em and I have a problem, Granddaddy Ed."

Dawn grabbed Ed's hand as he fiddled with the leather strap of a horse bridle and tugged him away from his job at hand.

"Let's take a seat over here by the stall and you tell me what's on your mind."

The girls hurried over to drop in the hay. Ed pulled over an abandoned stool. "What's up?"

Dawn glanced at Emily, and when she nodded, Dawn continued. "You know how my mom wants to get married so that I can be her legal daughter?"

"Yes, I'm aware of that."

"Okay, well, Em wants to help her father find someone to date. She's been real lonely for a mom."

Ed nodded. "Okay, I can see that."

"It seems pretty clear to us that my mom and Em's dad should get together. It would solve all our problems. Em would get a mom. We'd be an instant family."

"And Dawn and I would be sisters," Emily chimed in.

Ed rubbed his chin. "Let me see here—you two want to make a family?"

"Yes, sir."

"And you think Gabe and Lindsey would be the perfect parents?"

The girls nodded in unison.

"So what's stopping you from accomplishing that task?"

"Mom! She's planning on going out on dates with all these other guys."

"And Dad doesn't seem in a hurry to even start dating again."

"So as far as you figure it, the timing is off."

They nodded again.

"You think those two like each other enough?"

Dawn glanced at Emily again. "They kept looking at each other funny last night," Dawn confided. "Like Mom would look at Mr. Banner when he didn't notice."

"And Dad's eyes got real wide when he saw Miss Summer all dressed up. And when we dropped her off, he was real quiet, like he gets when he's thinking about important stuff."

Ed leaned back on the stool and crossed his arms over his chest. "Well, girls, seems to me we have to come up with a plan."

"We started one last night, but we need another."

Emily poked Dawn in the arm. "Yeah, especially since your grandmother has a plan of her own."

Ed's eyebrows rose. "Laurel Ann's in on this?"

"Not with us," Emily groused.

Dawn stared up at her great grandfather. "So how do we start?"

"Don't you worry your pretty heads none," Ed assured them. "Give me some time to think about it, and I'm sure we'll get this thing done."

Dawn jumped up to wrap her arms around Ed's neck. "Thanks, Granddaddy Ed."

He hugged her back, then pulled Em over. "Come here, punkin. Get in on this hug."

She smiled before joining the group hug.

"Yessiree, munchkins, we'll make this thing work."

"Hurry along, Lindsey. Jerry will be here any minute."

Lindsey wrestled with her pantyhose, cringing at her mother's terse tone. Why, she asked herself for the millionth time, had she agreed to go on another date so soon? She was barely over the Ron debacle and her mother arranges another night out.

"Get back on the horse," her mother had cheered her on.

"I'd rather be horseback riding in a thunderstorm than doing this again," Lindsey muttered, finally getting her hose in place. She hopped into a pair of flats, not willing to be uncomfortable tonight, even in the pursuit of true love. She'd learned her lesson on the last date.

Jerry had called to tell her the date was casual. He had tickets to a production at the Paineville Playhouse. The Paineville Players, nicknamed the Painful Players, were doing a rendition of *Midnight Summer's Dream*, and his sister, Vera, had the lead.

Fortunately, the players all kept their day jobs. Still, it was entertaining to see what the directorial vision would be for this play. In the last show Lindsey had attended, the director decided to give his own written play a "direction never seen in Paineville." Or anywhere else within a hundred miles. The poor man had the actors moving out among the audience, which, in itself, wasn't a bad idea. Except the players kept trying to randomly choose participants and drag them on stage to be serenaded.

The director hired music students from the local high

school for the orchestra and, although they played well, couldn't keep from laughing when Mavis Hart tripped on her way up the stairs to the stage, causing a domino effect through the actors and audience members on stage. Lindsey and Dawn had laughed till their sides hurt, then laughed some more when they returned home to tell Gramma the story. She and Mavis had an ongoing horticulture rivalry, with no one remembering exactly how it started, but had something to do with roses, so Gramma made sure the details made it into the Paineville Gazette.

Lindsey looked into the mirror and smiled. Who said small town life was boring?

"Lindsey!" came her mother's now shrill cry.

"I'm almost ready!" she yelled back. On final inspection of her gauzy white blouse with oversized sleeves and a fitted bodice tucked into a black skirt, she was complete. She refused to let her mother straighten her hair tonight, instead pulling it back so loose ringlets swept over her shoulders. One light spritz of perfume and she reached for the purse just as the doorbell rang.

"Here we go again," she muttered, determined to give Jerry and this date a chance.

An hour into the production, Lindsey felt her lids slowly drooping. Although Shakespeare's dialogue was witty and entertaining, the troupe just didn't have the delivery the play needed. She shifted, trying desperately to stay interested, since Jerry leaned over whenever Vera stumbled on her lines to whisper, "Isn't she great?"

Lindsey nodded her head and stifled a yawn. This night seemed to have hit a dead-end.

"Psst. Lindsey."

Lindsey straightened, trying to make out the direction of the stage whisper. Five seats into the row, she looked toward the middle aisle to spy a body, bathed in the glow from the spotlight above, waving to her.

"Granddaddy?"

"Yes," he answered in a loud stage whisper. "Can you come to the lobby?"

"Is something wrong?"

"I'll explain it to you out there."

"Is Dawn all right?"

Around her, folks started turning their heads and shushing her. She glanced at Jerry, his eyes wide as he stared back at her.

"Sorry, Jerry. Really, I am."

"Lindsey." Her grandfather's voice came louder and more urgent.

"Coming." She grabbed hold of her purse and started moving down the aisle. "Excuse me, I'm so sorry. Pardon me."

Ed took hold of her arm as she reached him.

"What's wrong?"

"Nothing's really wrong. I just need to talk to you."

"Let's go."

A voice from the stage followed them as they hurried to the back of the theater. "Please, continue your conversation in the quiet lobby. We wouldn't want to disturb you."

Lindsey slowly looked back, her face heating as she saw all eyes, from the audience to the actors on stage, including a teary-eyed Vera, staring right at her. Actually, that little speech was the best delivered line of the night.

"Sorry," she called out weakly, as her grandfather tugged her through the door.

"This better be good," she muttered, blinking in confusion as her eyes grew accustomed to the bright lights of the lobby.

"It isn't serious. It's rather, well, embarrassing."

"Mom!" Dawn ran over from the door, just as Jerry joined them.

Lindsey hugged Dawn. "I didn't know you were here."

Dawn glanced at Ed. "Didn't you tell her yet?"

"I'm trying." He tousled Dawn's hair before finishing his story. "Your father took us to the Super Wal-Mart. We got separated, and by the time we realized it, we went to the parking lot and your daddy's truck was gone."

"Daddy just left you there?"

"All alone?" Jerry chimed in.

Ed shrugged. "We don't know. I called the house and neither Dorothea or Laurel Ann have seen him. We were standing outside, trying to decide what to do next, when Gabe and Emily pulled up.

"We told them what was going on, and they gave us a ride over here to find you."

"Why didn't you just go home?"

A silent communication passed between Dawn and Ed. "We thought you could give us a ride home?" Dawn tried.

Lindsey placed her hands on her hips. "You know I didn't drive here."

"I brought her over to see my sister's premiere performance," Jerry clarified.

"Well, I'll be," Ed scratched his chin. "That's right. Our mistake. C'mon, Dawn, we'll go out to the pay phone and call home again. So sorry to butt in. We'll see you at home." He took the girl by the hand and led her outside. They walked to the public phone, and after depositing a quarter, Ed placed his call.

"Wait," Lindsey cried, following them into the warm night. "Jerry can give us all a ride."

A deep, very familiar voice sounded behind her. "No need."

She whirled around, coming face to face with Gabe, Emily at his side. Surprised, but happy, she tried to control the out-of-control beating of her heart. Suddenly the night took on a whole new color. Lindsey smiled, enjoying the burst of excitement that charged through her at Gabe's presence.

"I decided to park and see what happened with Ed and Dawn. I wouldn't dream of leaving them stranded," he explained, his lips quirked.

Lindsey saw a definite twinkle in his eyes and her heart leaped. He must have come straight from work, his dark blue T-shirt had a light coating of sawdust, as well as his jeans and boots. "I think I see a pattern here."

Gabe chuckled. "Oh, yeah? Em just had to go to Wal-Mart tonight, at a very specific time. Wouldn't even let me change out of my work clothes. Imagine my surprise when we ran into your family."

Lindsey turned to the guilty-looking group on the sidewalk, her pique turning to concern. "I still can't believe Daddy would just leave them."

Just then a white Mustang, with bright red, orange and gold flames painted along the sides, sped up to the curb. Lindsey narrowed her eyebrows in confusion. First Gabe, now her grandmother shows up?

"Ed Summer, just what do you think you're doing?" Dorothea climbed out of the driver's seat and chastised him. "We've been worried sick since you called. And where is William? I thought he took you to Wal-Mart in his truck."

"I expected him back before now," Laurel Ann cried as she exited from the other side of the Mustang. "I've been worried."

Ed held up his hands. "Look, it was all a misunderstanding. I'm sure William is fine."

Laurel Ann looked at her daughter and Jerry. "What on earth are you doing out here? You should be inside with your date." She spied Gabe and frowned.

"How did you know we were here, Greatgramma?" Dawn asked.

"Your Granddaddy Ed mentioned it when he left a message on my voice mail. Lucky I had my cell phone with me. We happened to be out anyway."

Ed had the grace to flush.

"Very subtle, Granddaddy," Lindsey said deadpan.

"Can we go back into the show?" Jerry asked, already taking Lindsey's arm.

"In a minute." Lindsey wasn't about to leave this group yet. They had major explaining to do. And more important, her pulse hadn't quite slowed down yet since Gabe's arrival. She wasn't about to give up the heady sensation to hear more garbled Shakespeare.

"Well I'm going in to catch the remainder of the play." Jerry scanned the crowd, muttered something about "crazies" and hurried back inside.

Lindsey sighed, secretly pleased at the turn of events. "Another potential mate bites the dust."

Gabe stood behind her, so close she could feel his body heat. He leaned forward and whispered for only her to hear, sending glorious shivers across her neck. "Jerry didn't seem too taken with your family. Not a good sign."

She turned her head and stared into his smokey eyes, drawn by the conviction there. Could it be possible that he didn't want her dating any other guys? Then why didn't he ask her out himself?

A big, black, King Cab pickup, with a large sticker emblazoned across the top of the windshield announcing to the world that Big Daddy had arrived, roared down the street, brakes screeching to a halt beside the small crowd. "Saints alive, Dad," William Summer said as he jumped from the truck and stormed toward his father. "You had me scared to death. By the time I realized the sales clerk at Wal-Mart sent me on a wild goose chase, you and Dawn were nowhere to be found."

"Uh, oh," Lindsey whispered.

"What wild goose chase?" Dorothea asked, her eyes narrowed and aimed right at Ed.

"When I got separated from those two, I went to the desk to ask that they be paged. I told the girl their names and she said that Ed had gone out to meet a friend who had a new car. She told me to meet them outside. By the time I got to the parking lot, no one was out there, so I figured they went for a ride in the new car. Then a buddy of mine came walking in and I asked if he'd passed you and he said he hadn't seen you or any car with you in it leaving the parking lot. So I got back in the truck, intending to look for you."

Ed flashed an innocent grin at the crowd. "Must have been some other old man who went for a drive."

Lindsey rolled her eyes at her grandfather's lame excuse. She heard Gabe stifle a laugh, then worried when she saw the gathering storm in her grandmother's eyes. Here stood a dead man walking.

"This is far from settled," Dorothea threatened. "Ed, get in the car."

William put his arm around Dawn's shoulders. "I think we should head home, young lady."

"Okay." She looked at him with guilty eyes. "Sorry, Papa. We didn't mean to scare you."

William visibly relaxed, another Summer family member completely smitten by Dawn. "I know, punkin. What do you say Em joins us and we go get a treat. I know it will make me feel better."

"Maybe Gabe has plans," Laurel Ann said as she

frowned at Lindsey, her meaning telegraphed loud and clear. *Don't mess this night up.* "We wouldn't want to keep him away from anything important."

"Looks like I'm free now." Gabe grinned at Lindsey and her stomach flipped.

"Lindsey," Laurel Ann cautioned as if she hadn't heard him. "Jerry must be waiting for you."

"No, Mom. I think that date is history."

"Then you should come home with us."

"Oh, please Grammy, let's go get that treat," Dawn begged. "Mom doesn't need to come. We promise to be good." She elbowed Emily and they both smiled innocently up at her.

One look at the girls' contrite faces and Laurel Ann caved.

After flashing Lindsey an annoyed glance, she led the way to the car, the girls following and high-fiving their victory.

In a mass exodus, everyone sped off into the night, leaving the echo of Laurel Ann's displeasure vaporizing in the night air.

Lindsey and Gabe were suspiciously alone, standing in the bright light of the overhead marquee.

Lindsey searched for the words to apologize. "I don't even know what to say after that . . . that . . . I don't know what to call it."

"How about a wreck on the side of the road. You know you should drive by, but you stop to look anyway."

She dropped her face into her hands. "My family," she moaned. "They mean well, really they do."

Gabe chuckled again.

She lifted her head. "I love them, but sometimes—"

"I come from the Banner family, remember? They're infamous for meddling."

She smiled at him, grateful that he was still with her and not running and screaming for the hills.

As at the library that one night, they were once again alone together. "Feels like deja vu," she said, peering around them at the empty street.

"And like the other night, you need a ride home."

"I don't think Jerry will be too keen on that job."

"I don't know about you, but I'm hungry. I just got off work a little while ago." He ruefully glanced down at his work clothes and brushed off the sawdust. "I'm not too bad off, but I don't think I'd get into the Magnolia Inn. And you're too dressed up for the Saucey Sow."

"Don't worry. I can't think of anything better than barbeque to end this night."

Gabe finished off the last rib, savoring the tangy barbeque sauce. "Guess we need to thank your family for dinner."

"If it wasn't for their interference, we'd have missed a great meal." Lindsey licked the remaining sauce from her lips.

Gabe froze, watching the innocent action. Lindsey had no idea just how attractive she was. And as he watched her, face flushed, laughing and enjoying herself, Gabe realized that he really did want to spend more time with her. On more than just these obvious setups. He wanted to date her. And as he watched her lips, he knew he wanted to kiss her.

Where had all the feelings come from? One minute he was happy to be back home, working with his brother, watching his daughter blossom, reunited with friends and family. And just as soon as he started spending time with Lindsey, he knew he wanted to be with her. Had known it for some time.

"Hey, where did you go?"

He started as Lindsey's voice interrupted his meandering. "Sorry. Just thinking about some things."

"Want to talk about it?"

No way. He still had to get a handle on being attracted to Lindsey. Besides, after tonight's fiasco, he doubted that she was ready to hear that he *might* be thinking about asking her out. Wouldn't that just make her feel special. No, he had to be sure before he took that step.

So, lawyer that he was, he changed the topic to something he could talk about. "I was thinking about Florida."

"Do you miss it?"

"No. This is home."

"You went down there for law school, right?"

He nodded. "Cindy wanted us to move there. A lot of her family already lived there, and her folks were getting ready to join them."

"Understandable. Most couples seem to live near the wife's family."

"Considering that my family was pretty . . . flexible, it seemed like the right choice."

Gabe's troubled parents had left the family when they were children, leaving them with Ruby Sue. The early years had been tough, financially and emotionally. They weren't exactly the most popular family in town. Ty and Marilyn had more trouble than he did with the loss, maybe because he was more pragmatic. He figured there was nothing he could do to change the circumstances, so he helped Gran instead of wishing for things to change.

That's me, he smiled to himself. Mr. Fix-it. Yet he couldn't fix the events of the accident that claimed the life of his wife.

Lindsey reached for a wet nap. "If this is too hard for you, we could change the subject."

"No, I guess I'm guilty of being a little too reflective at times."

"Hey, it's better than people who run on and on and talk about nothing."

"So you're saying you like the silent type?"

She blinked, her hands busy with the task of wiping off sauce, now still. "Um, yes, that's what I'm saying."

Gabe had to swallow a chuckle. She really looked good, here in the noisy restaurant, with music blaring and kids crying, yet she was composed and serene, listening to him. Composed, that is, until he turned the conversation to a more personal nature. Then he waited to see how she would react.

He liked what he saw.

She pushed her plate away. "It's getting late. We should probably head home."

He dropped a tip on the table and followed her out to the car.

When they were almost to her place, Gabe asked, "So, what's the plan?"

"Excuse me?"

"Well, this is the second date that started with you leaving with one guy and ended up with me taking you home."

"Oh my gosh, you're right."

"I think you need a better plan here. One that has you leaving and returning with the same guy."

She wrinkled up her nose. "I'm sure my mother has someone else lined up. She mentioned something about a friend of hers being in town tomorrow night."

"And you aren't ready for another date?"

"With the way things have been going, three strikes and I'm out."

Gabe laughed. He really loved her sense of humor. As

well as her company. The way she lit up whenever he was around. A guy could get used to that. The least he could do was help her out, right?

"Don't worry," she assured him. "I'll think of a way to get out of my mother's nefarious plans."

He took a deep breath and plunged into the idea that had been playing around in his head. "I can think of a pretty decent guy who isn't on her list."

"Really? Who?"

"Me."

Silence. Gabe glanced at her to make sure she was still with him. "Linds?"

"Did I hear you right? Are you asking me for a date?"

"Yes. I figure if I'm not on your mother's list, that will give you a break."

She stared out the window for a long minute. To his frustration, he found himself worried since she was taking so long to answer him. Just his luck, he asks a woman out for the first time in years, and she had to think up a nice excuse to shoot him down.

Finally she turned to him. "I'd like that," she answered in a small voice.

Despite his stubborn qualms, he said, "So would I."

Chapter Seven

Lindsey checked her watch for the third time. The literacy committee meeting she'd just come out of had taken longer than she planned. Realizing she was late, she bit down an impatient sigh. She still had to get home and change before Gabe picked her up.

A date with Gabe. Her heart did a funny little dance, even though he merely asked her out as a favor. How many years had she dreamed of this? Too many, if you asked her mother. She knew her mom meant well, wishing the woman still didn't hold the past against Gabe. But Lindsey wasn't going to let her mother ruin her night. She was ecstatic, walking on clouds, and Laurel Ann's dire predictions that this date was a mistake were not going to change her mind.

Shuffling the papers in her hand, she took one last look at the preliminary numbers for the cost of the Spring Gala fundraising dance. Lindsey concluded that everything was in order and laid the reports down on the library director's desk, just as she breezed into the office.

"So, what do you think?" Alanna Simmons asked. The

no-nonsense director of Paineville Library had become one of Lindsey's closest friends since the two met at the first literacy meeting a year ago. Lindsey knew she could depend on Alanna to help her get any job done, and Alanna knew that Lindsey would support any program the library needed. Together they made a pretty impressive team, and an added incentive was that they had fun together.

"Looks great to me."

"I know we need another meeting to nail down the particulars of the dance."

Lindsey gathered her purse and briefcase. "Just tell me the time, and I'll be there."

"So where are you off to in such a hurry? I haven't seen you much lately. Must be all the hot dates you've been busy with."

"Please," Lindsey shook her head. "Talk about a mistake."

"So what's up with the sudden dating, anyway."

"It's a long story, and right now I have to get going."

"Because . . . ?"

Lindsey smiled sheepishly. "I have a date."

"Another hot date?"

"No, *the* hot date."

Alanna leaned her hip against her desk, crossing slender arms over her chest. Petite, her blue-black hair, shaped in a short pixie cut, was styled in that messy, trendy look that Lindsey could never get away with. With gorgeous blue eyes and a complexion a model would die for, she presented the air of a woman who had confidence in her station in life. Her simple coral silk pantsuit completed her professional image. She certainly didn't fit the stereotype of your friendly neighborhood librarian. No, she exuded no-nonsense CEO to the max. Lindsey almost laughed, the after-hours, laid-back Alanna always relaxed in jeans and a T-shirt and didn't get much dressier than that.

"Okay, mysterious woman, give. Who are you going out with tonight?"

"Gabe Banner."

Alanna's mouth dropped open until she gathered her wits. "Are you kidding me? You better not be kidding me."

At Lindsey's affirmative nod, Alanna ran over to embrace her friend. "I can't believe this. It's just what you've dreamed of."

"I know, but he really just offered to help out with this dating dilemma I have."

"Dating dilemma? Oh, please," Alanna waved off Lindsey's comment. "I know you'll fill me in later on whatever the reason, so for now, just be yourself and Gabe won't be able to keep from falling in love with you."

Lindsey picked up her briefcase. "I'm not holding my breath."

Alanna gently pushed her towards the door. "Go on, get out of here. You have better things to do than hang around here when you need to get dolled up for Gabe."

"Wish me luck."

"I don't have to, you've got it made."

An hour later, Lindsey wondered if indeed, she did have it made. Laurel Ann had insisted on taking up Lindsey's time the moment she arrived home, going on and on about what a mistake it was to go out with Gabe, until Gramma, bless her soul, ran the woman out. Dawn kept coming in and out of the room, asking when Emily would be here. Finally, she was ready, but Gabe was fifteen minutes late.

He hadn't said where they would be going, so Lindsey had dressed in a pretty floral dress, one that flowed around her legs as she walked. She'd left her hair free, since the curls weren't too out of control tonight. This time, she did fuss over her makeup and secretly breathed a prayer that Gabe would appreciate the result.

She paced her living room, trying to work out the nervous energy. When that didn't work, she marched out to the porch to wait on the swing, only to find Gramma already there.

"I thought you went back to your house?"

"No, I wanted a few words with you, so I sent Dawn over so Ed could keep her busy. Although I don't know if I can trust those two together without supervision."

Lindsey laughed. "I'm sure Granddaddy knows better than to pull another stunt. I'm sure his ears are still ringing from the dressing down you gave him."

"Hmmph. He certainly deserved it." She patted the seat next to her. "Sit down, child."

Wary, Lindsey took a seat. She'd been getting way too much unsolicited advice lately.

"I want you to know that I approve of Gabe. He's a good man."

"Thanks, Gram."

"I think Gabe still grieves some for his late wife, but I also think that you are the woman that can make him see that love can come twice in a man's life. You both deserve a romance, a chance to feel the first stirring of love. The thrill you feel every time you see his face, and know that he is your special man."

"I don't know if he'd consider being my special man." She bit her lower lip and glanced over at her grandmother. "So you think I need to be cautious?"

"Cautious? Is that what you think? No, my dear, I want you to throw caution to the wind. Show the man that you're perfect for him. Let Gabe see that he'll never find another love like yours."

Lindsey pondered those words after her grandmother walked back to her own house. Should she show Gabe just what she felt in her heart? Would it scare him off? All along she thought she should be prudent, allow time to take care of this attraction between them. But take control? Lindsey wasn't sure just how to accomplish that, but the excitement in the pit of her stomach, just at the thought of Gabe being hers alone, urged her on.

The sound of a car coming up the drive announced Gabe's arrival. Lindsey banished the pre-date jitters to the back of her mind.

"Hi," Gabe called as he climbed out of the Lexus.

Emily exited the back and Lindsey pointed in the direction of Gram's house. After a quick good-bye kiss for her father, Em took off running.

Gabe strode toward the porch. "Sorry I'm late. We had a little last-minute drama at the Banner house."

"Nothing serious, I hope?"

"No, good news. My sister Marilyn just found out that she's going to be a mother."

A fleeting ache struck in the vicinity of her heart, but Lindsey made herself smile at his announcement. "Gabe, that's wonderful. She must be so excited."

"She is. And Dusty couldn't stop grinning." He frowned a little. "I don't know how we're going to survive two expectant Banner women at the same time."

"I'm sure Ruby Sue will take care of any problems."

"And Em and I will help out. I always wanted to have more kids, so I'll enjoy this family baby boom."

Lindsey frowned at his words, the old feelings of inadequacy welling up in her. She never, ever, once begrudged any woman the joy of having a baby. But here stood Gabe, admitting he'd like more children, the one thing she couldn't give him or any man. She swallowed the lump in her throat, refusing to dwell on any depressing thoughts while her dream date stood before her.

Gabe stopped at the steps, looking very handsome in a dark brown button down shirt tucked into tan slacks. He looked up at her, his smokey gaze catching and holding hers, upping her heart rate and making her suddenly warm.

He shifted and cleared his throat. Lindsey knew he was conscious of the rising temperature between them. She remembered feeling this way when they were kids, but attributed it to adolescent hormones. Now she was a woman, and still had the same physical reaction to Gabe. Breathless with nerves and wanting so much for him to do something as simple as hold her hand. No, her reaction to Gabe hadn't changed through the years, instead it had grown stronger.

"Ready?" he asked, his voice husky.

"Let me get my sweater." She hurried back into the living room, catching her breath. If this was a sample of how she was going to react to him tonight, she was in big trouble. *Fake date,* she reminded herself. *Fake date.*

Before long they were in the close confines of his car, headed toward town. "I know you've been on the dating merry-go-round, so I figured a quiet evening would be the ticket."

"How quiet?"

"For one, no kids. And second, I didn't tell a soul where I was taking you."

She grinned. "Sounds like an excellent plan."

"I thought so." He glanced at his watch. "Do you like the symphony?"

"Sure."

"I have two tickets for the show tonight. They're playing in Gainesville, so if I hurry, we'll make it just in time."

Lindsey settled back, knowing it would take a good forty-five minutes before they arrived at the auditorium. Which was fine with her. She wanted all the one-on-one time with Gabe as possible.

"Things sure have changed since you came back to town," Lindsey commented, trying for a familiar topic to start the lagging conversation.

He nodded. "I'm happy for my brother and sister. They had it tough growing up and now they're both happier than I've ever seen them."

"I know your family always kept a low profile after your mother left town."

"Ty and Marilyn really took her leaving hard."

"And you didn't?"

"Trust me, it hurt. We all felt abandoned by her. I guess I changed my attitude because of Gran."

"Because she's so tough in any situation?"

"No, as a matter fact, just the opposite. I came home from school one day to find her at the table in our tiny kitchen, crying over a stack of overdue bills. She tried to hide it when I came in, but I'd already seen her tears, and that hurt worse than Mom leaving. I sat down with her and she just sort of let all her fears and concerns out—she'd held them in for so long she would have burst if she couldn't tell someone. By the time we finished our conversation, I'd decided to get a job and help the family. I never told Ty about that afternoon, but I really pushed him to get an after-school job too. It was tough making ends meet, but we did it. United. As a family."

"So family means a lot to you?"

"I guess that's why I finally came home. I thought stay-

ing near the place Em remembered Cindy would be good
for her. Over time I could see I was wrong. And in case
you hadn't noticed, Em is a handful. I needed the help of
my family."

Lindsey swallowed hard, her admiration for Gabe growing even stronger. Family meant the world to him, just as
it did to her. And now, caught up in Risa's latest whimsy,
she needed someone solid like Gabe. He was really the
answer to her prayers. Problem was, he'd probably never
want to get serious if he knew she couldn't have children.

They were almost to the auditorium when the jarring ring
of Gabe's new cell phone interrupted the drive.

"Gabe here. Casey? Wait, slow down so I can understand
you."

At Gabe's concerned tone, Lindsey's maternal antenna
went up.

"Call the doctor. We're on the way." He hit the end
button. "Sorry, Linds, but we're going to have to turn
around. That was Casey on the phone and she needs my
help."

"Is she all right? The baby?"

"She's having cramps." He reached across to touch her
arm, creating shivers through her. "Ty had to go to Atlanta
on business today and he made Casey promise that she
wouldn't drive anywhere. She's only got a few months to
go, and Ty doesn't like to leave her alone. She tried calling
Marilyn, but couldn't get a hold of her. I hope you don't
mind the change in plans."

"Of course not. Casey needs you."

"Thanks for understanding."

Not quite thirty minutes later, they pulled up to a lovely
two-story farmhouse, a noticeably pregnant Casey standing
at the top of the stairs waiting for them. Lindsey's heart
went out to her. She appeared exhausted, her blond hair

pulled behind her taut, pale face. She rubbed her swollen belly in a circular motion.

"I'm so sorry to bother you," she said as they approached.

"Don't worry about it. Do we need to go to the hospital?" Gabe asked, his voice calm in light of the circumstances.

"No, thank goodness. The doctor said I'm experiencing Braxton-Hicks contractions. He said its pretty normal to get these false contractions at my stage of pregnancy."

Lindsey let out a relieved breath.

Casey sheepishly glanced at Lindsey, then Gabe. "I can't believe I ruined your date."

"Don't worry," Gabe assured her. "Lindsey's a trooper. We both wanted to be here."

The sound of "we" coming from Gabe's lips sent another erratic shiver through her. For so long she wanted to be a part of his life, and here she was, part of his "we." Her heartbeat went crazy again.

"We can always make the symphony another night," Lindsey assured him.

"Well, in that case, I'd really appreciate it if you could run to the store for me. Ty would have a fit if I go by myself, and you know he'd find out, he's got spies everywhere."

Gabe leaned close to Lindsey. "Don't let her fool you. Even though she gives Ty a hard time when he barks out his orders, she listens to him."

"Anyway," Casey narrowed her eyes at him. "I'm suddenly very hungry for Mostly-Marvelous-Muddy-Marshmallow ice cream."

Lindsey laughed. "I thought I was the only person on this planet who liked that flavor."

"Apparently there are at least two of you," Gabe deadpanned.

"So, will you make a run, Gabe? Please, please, please."

"Enough. You had me with the first please." He took Lindsey by the hand. "Would you mind staying with her, just in case she gets scared again?"

"No problem. But I'd suggest you go quickly. She's looking pretty serious about that ice cream."

He laughed and squeezed her hand. "Be back in five."

Her arm tingled from his touch, even after he let go. "We'll be here."

Gabe returned in record time. He found the women in the kitchen, chatting away. He grinned at how easily women seemed to be able to bond over things like ice cream.

"Your knight in shining armor has returned." In one hand, he held up the bag of ice cream. The Pastry Palace box dangled from the other.

Both women eyed the pink box, then him. "Okay, so you crave ice cream, I need eclairs. All this stress was getting to me."

He carried the desserts to the counter, then stepped back, his gaze lingering over Lindsey. He really hated to call off their date, but he was equally glad that she understood and didn't pout about the change in plans.

That was one of the things he was beginning to appreciate in Lindsey. Life threw her curves, but that just made her determined to straighten things out.

Like that whole crazy dating scheme, and her even crazier sister putting her in a tight spot. It was obvious to anyone who saw Lindsey and Dawn together that they adored each other. No amount of finagling on Risa's part would ever change that. But her demand that Lindsey marry, now that was over the top.

Lindsey deserved a guy who really loved her, who would

be there for her and Dawn. Someone who understood the importance of family, who knew how important roots were. It would take more than a two-time date to realize Lindsey was a wonderful and loving mother. This guy needed to know her, really know her. Her dreams and desires. Her fears and concerns. How deeply she could love. Lindsey needed a guy like . . . him.

He nearly choked on his thoughts. Good God, where did that come from? Granted, he'd known Lindsey most of his life, but he'd only just returned after years of absence between them. How could he think he knew her that well?

His gaze traveled to her and his heart pounded. She looked at home in this kitchen, laughing and eating ice cream while at the same time as alluring as he'd ever seen her. It occurred to him that he had thought more about her in the last week than any other woman he'd met. He had always tried to keep his mind occupied on the construction job or Emily's education, not wanting to dwell on his loneliness. He suddenly realized that recently he hadn't felt quite so lonely. Since he'd starting having run-ins with Lindsey, he'd been thinking about her non-stop. And enjoying every minute of it.

"Hey Gabe, why don't you join us before we get into your eclairs," Casey said as she emptied the Pastry Palace box and placed the eclairs on a plate.

Still stunned at his revelation, Gabe nodded absently. "Help yourself, Casey."

Lindsey regarded him with a quizzical expression, but he glanced away. Did he think he could solve Lindsey's problems? Just when he thought he had things settled in his life, he realized that he couldn't get comfortable. Life changed constantly, and if he wanted to enjoy the ride, he'd better just strap himself in and go for it.

His head accepted it, but he knew his heart would be a tad bit slower to give up the past.

Chapter Eight

By the time Ty came home, the trio had spent the evening playing Trivial Pursuit. Lindsey couldn't remember the last time she'd had so much fun. Not only were Gabe and Casey good sports, they were both incredibly smart. Lindsey kept trying to divert them from the game questions by asking about Casey's craft store or Gabe's job site.

Gabe stood after narrowly winning the last round. "I think we should head out, Linds. Casey probably needs some rest."

Casey awkwardly pushed herself from the couch, smiling up at her husband as he helped her up. "I hope I can hold out for another month."

"I don't think you have a choice, darlin'." Ty smiled down at his wife, his love so pure it brought a deep longing to Lindsey.

Covering her reaction, she said, "I really had fun tonight. Thanks, Casey."

"No, I'm the one who should be thanking you. I ruined your date to help me with a little false labor."

"It's fine, really."

"I owe you one." Casey lumbered over and hugged Lindsey. "Oh my goodness," she cried. "The baby is kicking. Feel it."

Casey grabbed Lindsey's hand and planted it on her belly. Lindsey felt the light flutters just as Casey tugged Gabe's hand and placed it besides Lindsey's. It was a beautiful and painful moment all at once. Slowly, she moved out of the way so Ty could feel his child's movements.

"C'mon, lets leave these lovebirds alone." Gabe handed Lindsey her sweater. "If I know those two, they'll be talking baby talk for hours. It's still early enough for us to do something."

They said their good-byes once again.

"So, do you have a location in mind?" Lindsey asked as they walked to the car, the twilight long giving way to the dark blanket of night. The wind lifted a strand of Lindsey's hair and she breathed in the scent of warm earth, along with the tantalizing fragrance of newly blooming lilies and violets. Feeling so gloriously alive, she asked herself just how much of her good mood had to do with the man walking beside her. When he opened the car door, she brushed by him, feeling his heat and strength, and realized he had everything to do with her good mood.

"As a matter of fact, I do have a place in mind. I think you'll like it."

"Then lead on."

After letting Lindsey in, Gabe rounded the car and climbed in, then headed the car in the direction of Half Moon mountain. With one of the highest peaks in the area, Half Moon loomed over Paineville.

Local legend proclaimed that when the first settlers of Paineville looked over the ridge on their first night in the area, they could only see half of the full moon that night. Hence the name. "There's a special place I'd like to take you."

"Sounds mysterious."

"Not really. But I think you'll like it."

Gabe drove expertly through the winding mountain roads, leading them further up the mountain. Lindsey didn't remember any place of importance up here, but trusted Gabe to keep his word. She tried not to put too much hope into the fact that Gabe wanted to take her to a special place, a place he wanted to share with her. She almost couldn't contain the joy of the moment, her heart beating with excitement and a silly grin on her lips.

Before long he slowed down and peered into the shadows. "I know the road is here somewhere."

"How can you see in the dark?"

"I'll know it by the mile marker." He squinted at the small sign on the side of the road. "Here it is." He pulled the sleek car onto a dirt road and drove into the depth of canopied trees.

"This can't be more than a wide path."

"I have to admit, it's been a while since I've been up here."

"You're going to scratch your paint."

"I'm not worried. Besides, up ahead there's an opening."

Lindsey could see a patch of star-filled sky before them that grew bigger as Gabe steered the car into a clearing. He parked and switched off the lights, giving them an unobstructed view of the enchanting scene spread out before them. Below, the lights of Paineville twinkled like fairy lights. Tiny windows in the houses below glowed with warm light while folks settled in for the night. Main Street beckoned with friendly street lamps.

Lindsey caught her breath as she stared out over the town

she'd been raised in, a place she never wanted to leave. "This is so beautiful. I feel like I'm in the movies. I didn't know this place existed. How on earth did you find it?"

"I stumbled across it in high school. When I finally saved enough money to buy a car, clunker that it was, I always went exploring. I'm not sure why, maybe to get away from the hard times at home. Anyway, I found this place by accident. After that, I came here whenever I needed to think or figure things out."

"You never seemed like you let things bother you. I remember thinking you were one put-together guy for a high school kid."

"No, I wasn't that secure." He opened his car door. "Let's go outside. The view is even better."

Lindsey stepped out into the warm night, lured by the promise of something elusive, something . . . "Magical," she exclaimed. "It's absolutely magical here."

"Magical, huh?"

She turned her head to get a glimpse of Gabe's somber expression. "What? You don't believe in magic?"

"Do you?"

"Sure, but I asked you first."

He chuckled. "I suppose some people could fall for a certain magic here. Maybe, if you're a kid."

"So you think only children see magic?"

Gabe leaned against the hood of his car, staring out at the town and the stars. Lindsey joined him, their world protected by tall oaks and maples, as well as mountain laurel shrubs. The fragrance charged the night air with the scent of new spring growth, and a sense of endless possibilities.

"I guess I stopped looking for magic a long time ago, but I want Em to have it in her life."

"She's a young girl. She finds magic daily."

The wind picked up, urging the tree limbs to clap in its wake. The night air brushed her skin, sending goosebumps up her arm. Or was that from Gabe's nearness?

"I should get my sweater." Lindsey started around the car when Gabe reached out to stop her. His firm fingers gently cupped her upper arm and he slowly, hypnotically, drew her to his side.

"No need." He wrapped his arm around her shoulder and tucked her close to him. "I'll keep you warm."

Lindsey closed her eyes, unable to get her pounding heart to slow its beating. Only in her most secret dreams had she ever been so close to Gabe. She had only imagined how his firm body would feel pressed to hers, how his masculine scent would fill her with heady abandon. Now she knew the reality and it far surpassed any hazy imagine she might have dreamed.

Too bad it was a fake date. She opened her eyes and grew tense at the sobering thought. Gabe was being a good sport, going along to help with Risa's demand. Lindsey didn't think for one minute that he wanted anything more serious than friendship. He'd had the love of his life. Why would he think about a new life with her?

"Hey. You don't need to be nervous with me."

That's what you think.

She took a breath and relaxed. "Sorry. To be honest, I never expected us to be . . . in this kind of situation."

"What situation? On a date or in a secluded clearing late at night with my arms around you?"

She shrugged, struggling to present an air of nonchalance that she didn't feel. It didn't work, so she admitted, "Both, actually."

"So is that good or bad?"

She stared up at him, his familiar face bathed in the moonlight. His handsomeness took her breath away. When her gaze met his, she glimpsed a fire banked there. What would it take to finally ignite the sensations flowing between them?

Slowly, leisurely, his gaze traveled to her lips. She tried to remain calm, but knew she was doing a poor job. Nervously, she licked her lips.

A flame flared in his eyes, and slowly, Gabe's lips settled over hers and it took all her willpower to not throw her arms around his neck and tell him how she had wished for this moment for all these years.

Which wouldn't be very smart, so she returned his kiss, glorying in his masterful touch and the wonderful sensations that wrapped around her and made her giddy inside.

An eternity later Gabe broke the kiss. He smiled at her, his smokey eyes missing none of the pleasure she was sure showed on her face.

"I've been wanting to do that for a while now," Gabe told her, his voice low and husky in the depth of the night.

"Really?" was all she could manage to croak out of her tight throat.

He nodded. "Let's try that again."

Lindsey leaned into him, grabbing a handful of his shirt to hold herself steady as she took her time exploring this next kiss. No, this was nothing like her dreams. This reality was a million times better.

"Wow," Gabe whispered against her lips.

"Yeah," she replied with a smile.

Lindsey rested her head on his shoulder, more content than she could ever explain, and didn't want to examine. She only knew it had to do with Gabe and she wanted to remain in this bewitching moment of time.

"Okay, so maybe some magic does exist," Gabe spoke softly against her hair.

"I suppose every person has to make the magic in their own life."

Gabe held her close and she breathed in his tangy aftershave, burning his essence to her memory.

"I've been thinking about your problem," Gabe mentioned idly, even though she could feel the tension flood his shoulders.

Lindsey stilled. "Which is?"

"Adopting Dawn."

"Ahhh—once a lawyer, always a lawyer. Do I have to remind you that you don't do law anymore?"

He laughed and hugged her closer. "No, not from the legal angle. From the family angle."

She twisted to get a clear vision of him. "Come again?"

He took a deep breath, as if to fortify himself as he went on. "Em needs a mother figure. Your sister thinks you need a husband. We could solve both of our problems by becoming a family."

She pulled from his embrace to gape at him, her heart aflutter. The buzzing in her ears made her question what she thought she heard. "Are you asking me to marry you?"

"Well, that would make us a family."

"This is only our first date."

"True, but we've known each other for years."

"*Knew* each other. It's been a long time since we really spent any time together. So much has happened in our lives, so much has changed since we were kids."

"Not as much as you think. You're still the same, sweet Linds I remember."

"Is that what you really want? To be married again?"

He frowned, a flash of uncertainty passing over his face.

Lindsey swallowed the disappointment of Gabe's intent. She'd always wanted to be a wife and mother, but not like this. And in her dreams when she thought about marrying

Gabe, she wanted him to love and cherish her. Right now he couldn't even say the M word.

"Do you love me, Gabe? A romantic kind of love?"

His answer came from the deep frown on his forehead.

"I don't think so, Gabe. You're obviously not really convinced about this and I don't want my sister's demands to make you feel like you have to come to my rescue." She took a step away, putting much needed distance between them, forcing her tone to be light. "Besides, when I do get married, I want bells and whistles and a man who can honestly say he loves me."

Gabe nodded and stared out into the night. After a few minutes he removed his keys from his slacks. "I guess I should take you home."

"Please."

On the drive home, Lindsey clasped her hands firmly in her lap, repeating over and over that she wouldn't cry. Her mother was right. She was crazy to think Gabe would love her, not after having an idyllic marriage. He wanted less than she would accept for herself.

Just before she exited the car, Gabe tentatively touched her arm. "We're still friends?"

"Sure," she answered, her voice shaky. She had to get in the house soon before she made a fool of herself and started to cry in front of him. She ran up the steps and turned the key in the lock as he backed down the driveway. Then she went inside, slid down the closed door until she sat on the floor, hot tears rolling down her face as she silently called herself every kind of fool for believing in magic.

The bright sunlight burned Lindsey's eyes as she opened them the next morning. With a groan, she remembered the previous night and pulled the pillow over her head.

"This isn't going to work," she muttered, dragging herself out of the tangle of covers. She headed for the kitchen, bleary eyed, and stunned to her toes to find her sister Risa sitting at the pine kitchen table, a cup of coffee at her elbow as she flipped through a magazine.

"Hey, sleepy head. About time you woke up. Late night?"

"Yes, no thanks to you."

"Yeah, Mom told me about the dating marathon." Risa grinned, a satisfied gleam in her lovely eyes.

Lindsey wanted to snarl at her sister, but just couldn't work up the energy. Instead she poured herself some coffee and made herself busy by finding the cream and sugar so she could think of what to say. Not only was she surprised to see Risa, but to make matters worse, the girl sat there with her perfectly coifed hair and designer outfit, looking as confident as any model in the fashion magazine she held.

On the contrary, Lindsey looked and felt like she'd been given the once over by a manic hairdresser and spaced-out costumer. Her hair stuck out in every imaginable angle and beneath her worn and tattered robe she wore an oversized T-shirt and baggy socks. Beauty and the Beast. Risa being the beauty, of course.

"So why are you here? More ultimatums?" Lindsey snapped.

"Ohh, someone got up on the wrong side of the bed."

"Wrong side of my life," she grumbled.

"Speaking of life, I wanted to fill you in on what's going on in mine," Risa enthused as she braced her elbows on the table, smiling as if she didn't have a clue to the mess she'd made of Lindsey's life.

Lindsey gave her the evil eye.

"You see," Risa continued blithely, ignoring Lindsey's glare, "I'm getting married."

Getting hit with a fifty-pound bag of cement couldn't have rocked Lindsey's world more than her sister's announcement. "Repeat that?"

"I'm getting married."

Lindsey's knees buckled and she sank into the chair across the table from her beaming sister. "I thought you swore off marriage after you and Tommy broke up."

"That was before I met Baxter."

"Baxter who?"

"Baxter Carlyle, the third."

"The third what?"

"Carlyle, of course."

"Of course." Lindsey drank some coffee. "And he is who, exactly?"

"Well, his family owns a chain of restaurants. I met him when I was staying in Atlanta about a year ago. We ran into one another at social functions and hit it off. Before long he wanted to get serious, but I still wanted to run. You know how I am about commitment."

Didn't she? After all the years she'd spent in limbo waiting to get custody of Dawn?

Wait. Something didn't compute here. Risa at social functions? She didn't stay in one place long enough to find out where any social functions were actually held. Not to mention that the type of function her sister would show up for was probably not the best place to find a decent, marriageable man.

"Where did you really meet him?"

Risa colored and looked away. "Okay, if you must know, I was working at Boomers."

"That restaurant notorious for biker fights and harassment suits?"

"Yes," Risa snapped in return, her blue eyes suddenly stormy. "Baxter was there with friends. We hit it off. He asked me out, and before I knew it, I quit that dive and he asked me to marry him. I had to think about it."

"For a year?"

"Hey, I want to be sure before I get married again. I don't want to rush into it again, marriage is a big commitment."

"But it's okay for you to force me to rush into getting married so I can have Dawn?"

Risa's shoulders slumped. "No, it's not."

Lindsey sighed. "Okay, so you're getting married. What else should we know?"

"It's about Dawn."

Lindsey's stomach took a serious swan dive. Her palms grew moist as she remained calm until she heard the news.

"You see, Baxter is a bit older than me. He doesn't want any children. That's why I took so long getting to know him. I wanted to see if he would take Dawn in and we could be a real family. But as time went on, I realized he wasn't interested in children. He has other interests." Risa bit her lower lip for long seconds. Lindsey could have sworn she saw tears misting her sister's eyes, but then Risa had missed her calling as an actress. "The thing is, I really love him. I know, for the first time in my life, that this is right."

"So why demand that I get married? We've been doing fine just the way we are."

"Because Dawn needs a father. An entire family. I realize that now. And since I can't give that to her, you have to."

Lindsey rubbed her throbbing temples. "I'm getting a serious headache."

"When I heard that Gabe Banner had come back to town, I knew he was the perfect man for you. You've always been in love with him. And when I found out that Dawn and Emily are best friends, I couldn't imagine anything more perfect."

Lindsey glared at her sister. "You weren't specific in the man."

"Well, it was bad enough I had to do this. And I couldn't tell Mom, knowing how she feels about Gabe. I figured you and Gabe would find each other and it would all work out."

"Sorry to burst your bubble, but it won't work. If I get married, I want the man to love me. Gabe doesn't love me."

"Are you sure?"

"Yes. More than sure. Convinced. Resigned. These words practically came from his own mouth."

"Ouch."

"Yeah."

Lindsey pushed her chair from the table and rose to look out the window. Fresh tears blurred her vision. Funny, after last night, she didn't think she had any tears left to cry.

"This is not good. It changes everything."

Lindsey spun around. "What do you mean?'

"I need you to get married fast, and then you can have Dawn. That doesn't change. Baxter wants to get married this summer. We're planning a big, outdoor wedding and reception at the family estate. I can't have you show up with Dawn and no husband. I don't want Baxter to suspect a thing."

Lindsey's ears perked up at Risa's statement. She didn't want Baxter to know about Dawn and Risa? Whoa, here.

"Does Baxter even know about Dawn?"

"Not exactly," Risa hedged.

She shouldn't be shocked, really, but Lindsey had thought maybe her sister had finally grown up.

"So, as I was saying, we've only got a short time to get

you married." Risa stood and walked to Lindsey's wall calender to examine the months. "That's it." She pulled the calender from the wall and carried it to Lindsey. "Here we go. The Spring Gala dance. If you're engaged that night, I'll let you adopt Dawn."

"And if I'm not? You don't want Baxter to know about Dawn, so you can't force me into anything. Besides, how can you even consider marrying this man and not tell him about Dawn? You think he won't find out?"

"I'll make sure he doesn't find out?"

"Risa, think about this. Of course he'll learn the truth eventually."

Tears glistened in Risa's eyes. "I really need you to go along with this. I don't want to do this, but I'll let Mom and Dad adopt her if you won't help me."

A sharp pain stabbed Lindsey's chest. "You wouldn't!" she whispered.

"I need this, Lindsey." Tears ran down her cheeks. "Please, get engaged by the the gala. And I won't ask you for another thing, I promise."

Dawn backed away from her hiding place just beyond the kitchen door and stealthily hurried to her bedroom. She brought the phone with her as she hid beside her bed, listening for either Risa or Lindsey to walk down the hallway. Once she felt the coast was clear, she called Emily.

"Risa's here and I'm afraid she's going to ruin everything."

"Try not to worry."

"I can't help it. Every time she shows up here, Lindsey is upset."

"I think it's time to move to plan B."

"We haven't got a plan B. We didn't think we'd need it."

"Let me talk to Great Gran. She'll come up with some-thing."

"And I'll talk to Granddaddy Ed."

"Make sure your grandmother isn't around. She keeps messing up our plans."

"Right."

"Do you think we still have a chance?" Em whispered.

"Like Greatgramma says, you have to make your own luck."

"And we have to make our own family, Dawn. Just you wait and see. We're going to get what we want."

"Then cross your fingers."

"And pray, hard."

"Amen," Dawn answered.

Chapter Nine

Gabe knew he messed up. Of course, it didn't take a genius to figure that out, but he still felt crummy about last night. What had he been thinking? Asking Lindsey to marry him?

Sitting and swaying on the front porch swing did little to really help him come up with answers, but the sweet morning air had drawn him to sit and contemplate his fate with Lindsey. He stared out over the rolling land, up to the dark mountains and felt a sense of home. Of belonging. At least some things in life felt good.

Well, he hadn't actually come right out and asked her to marry him, but she knew what he meant. He only wanted to help her out of a sticky situation, to be useful again. Mr. Fix-it.

She'd known. She recognized the offer as a business deal, not a romantic proposal. He'd seen it in her eyes. And wasn't that the worst part? She knew and understood that he wasn't sure if he was capable of giving her more, yet even with the hurt evident on her lovely face, she turned him down gently and with dignity.

Ty was right about the sparks. Oh, yeah, he felt them last night. Once he ruined the mood, it took all his strength not to grab her by the shoulders and haul her lips to his for another amazing kiss. He was sure the sparks between them would have lit up the dark night.

But Lindsey was right. He hadn't given her any reason to think she was special to him. She deserved a guy, who loved her. A guy who would put her first in his life. A guy who wouldn't confuse the need for an intact family with a marriage proposal.

A guy who needed to get out of the past.

He ran his hand over his face and groaned out loud.

She looked great last night. To say otherwise would have been an understatement. He couldn't take his eyes off her. He loved her ready smile, the easy way she laughed. He thought about the kiss they'd shared last night and realized he wanted to kiss her again. And again. He still savored the way her soft body had melted into his, how right he felt with his arms around her.

But after his tactical error last night, he wouldn't be surprised if she never spoke to him again.

Ruby Sue came out to join him on the porch, taking a seat beside him on the hanging swing. Her slight weight barely caused the swing to move.

"So, you messed up your date last night?" she asked without preamble.

"How'd you guess?"

"I have eyes, boy. You're moping around, drinking coffee and staring out over trees."

He sighed. "Yeah. I messed up."

"Nothin's ever bad enough that it can't be fixed." She gave him a reassuring pat on the knee.

He grinned. Gran never saw any circumstance with a down side. Her motto: Always search for a solution.

"I'm not sure about that."

"Lindsey is a reasonable girl. Go talk to her."

"That's the problem. I did enough talking last night to stick my foot in my mouth. I don't think she wants to hear anything I have to say right now."

"We Banners can't be accused of thinking and talking right when it comes to love."

Gabe's jaw fell. Love? What on earth . . . "Hold on, Gran. I didn't say I was in love with Lindsey."

"No, no you didn't, but you sure act like it."

"How can you . . . I never said . . ." He stopped before he proved Gran right.

"Uh, huh, just like I said. No Banner can ever think right when it comes to love."

"Gran, I haven't seen Lindsey in years. We're just getting reacquainted." He silently groaned at his words. Lindsey had said the same thing the night before. "And besides, I don't know if I want to fall in love again."

"Gabe, I know it's been a tough few years. And I know you're havin' a hard time lettin' go of the past. But let me tell you something. The past don't keep you warm at night when you sleep in a big bed all by yourself. The past can't be a mother to Emily. And the past has no place in the future. Your future."

Gabe stared down at his cooling coffee. "I know that Gran. Believe me, I've told myself that very thing."

"Then what're you afraid of?"

"Afraid of?"

"Yes, I see fear, plain and simple, all over your face."

Should he say the words out loud? The words that would bring to life the thoughts he'd refused to dwell on for so long? They were there, deep inside him, but he'd refused to acknowledge their power. Maybe if he said the words, the fear wouldn't have power over him anymore. *If* he said the words.

He glanced at Ruby Sue, who sat serenely watching birds jump from one budding branch to another, her hands folded primly over the apron tied over a simple cotton dress. She'd been through so much in her life; raising three kids alone, overcoming the stigma of being poor trash, and conquering her fears. And she knew him well enough that he guessed she already knew what his fears were. She also knew he had to voice them to move on.

He took a deep breath. "I couldn't help Cindy when she needed me most. Because of it, she died. I can't go through that again. Heck, I'm barely there for Emily."

Ruby Sue reached out her gnarled hand and took his hand in hers. "You know there're no sure things in life, boy. Each day we open our eyes, get out of bed and live our lives. Some days are better than others.

"But God don't give us more than we can handle. I don't know why Cindy died. Why Em couldn't grow up knowin' her mama. But that doesn't change things. You can't be afraid to live, Gabe. And you've got to learn that you can't control everything. That's life."

Gabe closed his eyes, letting the weight of his grandmother's words sink deep into his soul.

"It's still so hard, Gran. Even when your words make sense."

"Nothing worth havin' is easy."

Gabe opened his eyes and chuckled. "That's what Ty said."

"I taught him well."

He looked at Gran to see a wealth of strength gazing back at him. If she could handle what life had dealt her, didn't he at least owe it to himself to give it a try?

"Lindsey's worth it," Gran told him as she smoothed the frayed collar on the old shirt he'd put on to wear to work today.

Yes, she is, he thought to himself, not sure if he could agree to much else just yet.

Lindsey glanced at her watch, shocked to see how much time had passed. Although she'd been here for two hours, it seemed as if she'd just arrived at the library, her sanctuary away from her meddling sister, nosy mother, concerned grandparents and unhappy niece. Instead of dealing with problems head-on like she normally would, Lindsey needed to escape the pressures of home but wasn't in the mood to drive to town, so she hitched a ride with her father, the one family member who didn't require anything from her. For a few hours, she'd concentrate on the spring dance, as well as go over her literacy presentation with Alanna.

She gathered together her notes as Alanna rejoined her after attending to yet another library emergency.

"What a day," said her perky friend, who dropped into a chair across the table from Lindsey. "I'm sorry I didn't get to spend more time with you. Saturday afternoons are usually busy around here."

"You didn't miss much, but thanks for the concern. I really needed the quiet time."

"Tough date last night?"

Lindsey's head came up. "What do you mean?"

Alanna shrugged, visibly keeping her curiosity in check. "When you didn't rush into my office this morning singing Gabe's praises, I figured something went down."

"It wasn't a bad date, as dates go."

"You are the expert right now."

Lindsey grimaced. "Please, don't remind me."

"At least you have dates," Alanna complained.

Lindsey grinned. "So would you if you didn't turn every guy down who asks you out."

Alanna's face grew somber. "I have my reasons."

"And some day you'll tell me."

"We were talking about you. And Gabe."

"He offered to marry me."

"What?" Alanna jumped up from the chair to stare at Lindsey.

Lindsey held up her hand. "Don't get all excited. It was nothing romantic. He only thought he could help me get custody of Dawn."

Alanna slowly lowered herself back into her seat and Lindsey continued. "Besides, I don't want him sacrificing his life because he's a noble man. This is my dilemma."

"True, but he'd didn't have to ask you. It's not like you forced him or anything."

"I know." Her shoulders slumped. "I want romance. Flowers. Declarations of undying love."

Alanna dropped her chin into her upraised palm. "Don't we all."

"And with this mercenary dating schedule my mother has me on, I'll never find that. And keep Dawn."

"Hey, where's Miss Optimistic? You always see the good side of every situation. Just hang in there. The right man is out there for you."

But I want the right man to be Gabe. "I don't know anymore."

"Gabe really got you down last night, didn't he?"

"And then Risa greeted me this morning when I woke up. She upped the deadline."

"No way."

"Yes. She has her reasons, and so her threat level has moved the timetable to the Spring Gala."

"So what are you going to do?"

"I don't know, Alanna, I really don't know." She zipped the briefcase, stood, and laced it over her shoulder. "So for now, I'm going home to take a long, hot bath. Maybe I'll be struck with inspiration."

"Good luck, honey. If you need anything, just give me a call."

"Deal."

Lindsey meandered around the tables, passing rows of bound treasures placed in symmetrical lines along the massive shelves. She inhaled deeply, loving the smell of books, mingled with the age of the old building and the creaky wood floors.

Her passion had always been reading. In college, she volunteered for a literacy program as part of a course she was taking, and found herself deeply moved by the hard work many folks went through to learn to read. When she came back to Paineville, she continued the volunteer work at the local library and through the years had worked to build the volunteer base. After trial and error, she'd come up with a practical literacy program a few years back, and with the help of Alanna, it was adopted in many counties. She even had the backing of the governor. If all went well, her program might move state-wide.

Which really would have excited her, had it not been for her personal predicament. She crossed the main foyer and headed out into the warmth of late afternoon sun, scanning the parking lot for her father's monster truck, but he hadn't arrived yet. Deciding to enjoy what was left of the wonderful spring day, she sat on the cement landing that flanked the steps leading to the main entrance and turned her face up toward the sun. The rays warmed her skin as a breeze lifted the ends of her hair. She smiled and relaxed in slow degrees.

"Wherever it is you've escaped to, I'd like to come."

Lindsey jerked at the sound of Gabe's voice, lifting her lids while controlling her suddenly erratic heartbeat. So much for a moment of relaxation.

"What are you doing here?"

"Disturbing your solitude, you mean?"

She smiled in spite of herself, in spite of the fact that he'd just about broken her heart last night. "You're like The Shadow. You seem to always know where to find me."

Gabe chuckled. By the looks of him, he must have just finished up at the job site. Sawdust still clung to his dark hair. "Nothing mysterious to it. Em called to let me know that she was staying to have dinner with your family, and your grandmother got on the phone and invited me over. I heard your dad in the background saying that he was about to pick you up, so I offered since I'm going that way."

Lindsey tried to fume at her meddling family, but couldn't build up a good head of steam. Gabe always took her breath away before she had a chance to go off. Even if he couldn't get serious with her, she couldn't deny that he made her heart race. How could she stay mad at him?

"I guess that'll save Daddy a trip to town."

"If you don't mind, we'll just swing by home so I can take a quick shower and change. Ty and I got carried away on the job site and I don't want to go out looking like a mess."

Lindsey's gaze dropped to his clothes. He was right, he was a mess. Mud covered his boots, splotched his legs and caked the hem of his jeans. His blue work shirt was patterned with streaks of mud and sawdust.

"What did you guys do?"

He held up a hand. "You don't want to know. Rest assured that no animals were injured in the raising of Buddy Lee's collapsed stable, although I became intimately acquainted with a pile of manure."

She picked up his scent on the wind and wrinkled her nose. "You're right, you do need a shower."

He flashed her a lazy smile that made her temperature rise. "Thanks for noticing, ma'am."

She couldn't help but laugh. Here he was, covered with mud and who knew what else, and he joked about it. He didn't look the least bit embarrassed by the aroma radiating from him.

"Just pinch your nose when we get in the truck."

"What, no Lexus?"

"Ty had pity on me and sent me home with his truck."

"So Ty didn't—"

"Fall in the muck? No. The rat managed to come away clean. He's bringing my car to Gran's."

She grabbed her briefcase. "Let's get going before you attract any flies or whatever."

"You're not really showing much sympathy to my plight," he said as they walked to the truck.

"Hey, buddy, Granddaddy raises animals. I've smelled worse."

He laughed again, his eyes crinkling with real humor. Mud and whatever notwithstanding, Lindsey still thought he looked wonderful. His eyes. It had to be the eyes. So gray and deep, so compelling, he could glance at her and she'd follow him anywhere. The Pied Piper of Paineville.

"What're you smiling about?"

"Nothing."

He started the ignition and began to drive through town. "You better not be mocking me."

"Me? Mock? I'd never do that." She bit the inside of her cheek.

"Remember. Paybacks."

"Oh, that's scary coming from a man who could send

wild animals fleeing for their lives just from the smell of you."

Gabe grinned and drove.

Leaning out the open window, Lindsey enjoyed the warm spring air, humming along with a Toby Keith tune playing on the radio. Last night made her realize that Gabe may not be serious about marriage, but today, in the practical sunlight, she at least could enjoy her dreams of a relationship with the man.

They had just reached the outskirts when Gabe squinted as he peered out the window. "What the heck?"

Lindsey followed his gaze, groaning when she realized what he was looking at. Her granddaddy Ed motored into town, bouncing along on his John Deere tractor. When the truck passed, Ed gave a jaunty salute. Gabe gaped at him, then at her.

"Gramma hid his truck keys," Lindsey explained, "because he won't wear his glasses. She's afraid he'll cause a wreck and he's too stubborn to admit his vision is bad. So he embarrasses her by driving the tractor into town."

Oh—kay," Gabe answered. "In a weird way, it makes sense."

Lindsey felt the color rise in her face. She hadn't thought her family could possibly find one more way to embarrass her when Gabe was around, but once again, someone had. Thankfully, Gabe didn't say another word until they reached his grandmother's house.

"We'll go around back. Gran will skin me alive if I come in the fancy front foyer smelling like this."

When they entered, they found Ruby Sue sitting at the kitchen table, peeling potatoes. She looked Gabe up and down and winced. "Lord have mercy, boy, what have you got into?"

"Buddy Lee's horse pen. We were trying to fix the side of the stable that had collapsed during the winter. Once we had the wall up and supported, I climbed on the outside of the adjoining wall, slipped on the ladder and fell right into the thick of things."

Ruby Sue listened to his story slack-mouthed. Lindsey bit back her need to laugh.

"Now, if you ladies will excuse me, I'm going to get cleaned up." He narrowed his gaze. "Gran, behave."

"Watch who you're talking to, boy."

"I should come over there and plant a big kiss on your cheek."

She held up the paring knife in defense. "Not if you want to take Lindsey home in one piece, you won't."

He laughed at her threat and disappeared into the laundry room.

"Don't suppose his state bothered you?"

"I've been around Granddaddy too often. Not much fazes me when it comes to animal smells."

"Good. Gabe needs a friend like you." Ruby Sue nodded toward the wooden chair opposite hers across the large kitchen table. "Have a seat."

"Can I help?" Lindsey asked as she sat down.

"Thanks I'd appreciate that." Ruby Sue rose to retrieve another peeler, handing it to Lindsey as she took her seat.

Before she started her task, Lindsey gazed around the heart of the house, trying to form an impression of how much home meant to Gabe. She smiled. There was such a strong sense of belonging here, so much so that Lindsey had to admire what Gabe's family had overcome to get to the place they enjoyed today. Even though he didn't say much about their past, she realized how tight the Banner group must be, to stick together and come out with respect and love for each other. Family. The glue holding their lives together.

She picked up the peeler and started at the job at hand, holding back a heartfelt sigh. How much she wanted that with Dawn. And she wouldn't lie to herself and not admit she'd like to see Gabe and Emily in the equation. But as much as she wanted and needed her own family, love had to be the top priority. She wouldn't settle for less.

"So, you must be excited with all this great-grandbaby news," Lindsey offered, starting a conversation to take her mind off her problems.

The older woman's expression softened. "I've waited a long time for my grandchildren to get to this point. You can bet I'm beyond excited."

"We spent the evening with Casey and Ty last night. I don't think I've seen a happier expectant mother or a devoted father-to-be."

"That's Ty, he'll hover till he makes Casey crazy. Course I expect Dusty to pretty much act the same with Marilyn."

"It's amazing what babies will do to people."

"Makes us one big family, and I couldn't be prouder of my clan."

A short silence fell before Ruby Sue started asking after Lindsey's family and the literacy program at the library. Lindsey answered, but she knew it was just a matter of time before Ruby Sue turned the conversation toward the personal. She hoped Gabe would hurry along.

"Do you have an escort for the gala yet?"

Oh, no, here it comes.

"No. I've been so busy with the planning stages, I haven't gotten that far."

"Gabe likes to dance."

"Really? I didn't know that."

"He's also not adverse to being asked out by a woman."

"I'll remember that." *Gabe, where are you?*

"Emily has been spending a lot of time at your family's place."

"Does that bother you?"

"Not one bit. As long as you and Gabe keep an eye on them girls. At that age, there's no tellin' what mischief they can come up with."

Was that a friendly warning or just grandmotherly advice? Probably both.

Finally, loud footsteps sounded on the back stairs leading into the kitchen. Gabe appeared, freshly showered and dressed casually in a snug blue-patterned pullover shirt and khaki slacks.

He smiled at Lindsey and she nearly sighed aloud with dreamy longing. "Hope I didn't take too long?"

"No. Your grandmother and I were having a fine time chatting."

He glanced at Ruby Sue, humor in his eyes. "You didn't scare her off?"

"What did you think I'd do? Tell her that you two need to stop walking on eggshells and just admit what you feel for each other?"

Lindsey's eyes grew wide and she felt her face heat. Gabe, on the other hand, walked over to his grandmother and hugged her.

"That's what I love about you. You just say what you think."

Ruby Sue hugged him back, then broke the embrace and waved him off. "Go on, now, don't keep Dorothea waiting. I taught you better manners than that."

"Yes, ma'am."

Still smiling, he turned to Lindsey. "Let's go. The girls are probably wondering what happened to us."

She nodded and stretched out her hand to Ruby Sue. "It was a pleasure to see you."

"Next time Dawn wants to come over, you're more than welcome to join her. We can sit down and chat some more."

Gabe ushered her out the door and down the steps, leading her to the Lexus. Still embarrassed by Ruby Sue's words, she decided not to bring up the topic of anyone's "feelings," least of all hers for Gabe.

"You clean up nice," she told him as they walked to the Lexus which Ty had returned for his truck while Gabe showered. "I have to admit, when you dress nice you look more lawyerly."

"Is that a word?"

"Probably not, but it fits here."

He chuckled and helped her into the car. "That's me, dual personality."

She slid into the passenger seat, and when Gabe joined her, the space in the car suddenly shrank in his presence. The new-car leather smell mixed with his cologne created a heady mixture. Lindsey pressed the button to lower the window, needing fresh air to clear her senses before she did something crazy like lean over and kiss Gabe.

Gabe headed out toward the Summer compound, passing through downtown Paineville in the process. When he turned down Elm Street, and Lindsey saw a FOR SALE sign on the front lawn of a two-story Victorian house, she gasped out loud.

"What's wrong?"

"The Olsen house is for sale."

"Yeah, it just went on the market. Mr. Olsen hired Ty to do some renovations. We start next week."

"I love that house," she whispered in a wistful tone, thinking about her fantasies of living there. When she realized she might give herself away, she asked, "Do you know if anyone has shown interest in it yet?"

"I'm not sure. I could find out."

She half turned in her seat as the car passed by, her dream house fading into the distance.

"So, you like that house?"

She faced Gabe. "I always have, since I was a little girl. I used to ride my bike into town and come here and imagine living in that grand old house."

"That grand old house needs some major work."

She shrugged. "When you're a kid you don't care. It's the fantasy that counts."

"So, why don't you put a bid on it?"

Why not? It wasn't that simple. Not with the future in such turmoil. "I don't think so."

"Can't leave the family compound?"

"Believe me, there are some days I'd love to do just that."

"Then go for it."

She shook her head. "No, there are some dreams that stay just that, dreams. Some lucky family will move in there and be very happy, I just know it."

Gabe glanced at her, his enigmatic gaze capturing hers. He didn't say a word, yet Lindsey felt like he had stolen all her hidden dreams by merely looking into her eyes.

"Some dreams come true."

"Not my dreams," she whispered to herself.

Ten minutes later they arrived at her grandparents' house. Multiple cars in the driveway warned her of other guests. Lindsey could smell barbeque before she saw the smoke rise off to the side of the house. Her father definitely had his super-charged charcoal grilling machine cleaned up and ready for the first cook-out of the year. He loved that thing and tried to grill dinner every chance he got.

She heard children laughing as they ran around the yard, and saw her grandmother carrying a large platter of tomatoes and lettuce out to the table in the yard.

"Someone must be having a party," Gabe remarked.

Lindsey got out of the car, a smile tipping her lips as she looked across the roof at Gabe. He smiled back and suddenly Lindsey wished her dreams could be possible. That maybe in Gabe's circumstance, patience was a much needed virtue she had to honor in order for him to see her as more than a friend.

He continued to gaze at her, and once again heat rose on her skin and her heart's tempo picked up a racing beat. He drew her to him so naturally, as if they had always been together. She closed the door and started walking to him when her mother's voice rang out behind her.

"Lindsey, I'm so glad you're back. Look who came all the way down from Asheville, your old friend, Mike Post."

Chapter Ten

Gabe exited the car and frowned as Laurel Ann, her arm entwined through Mike's, strolled toward the car. When Lindsey shrieked and ran to Mike, flinging herself into his arms, Gabe caught his breath like he'd been sucker-punched.

"What're you doing here?" Lindsey cried.

"I have a couple of shows scheduled in the area, so I decided to come check on the homestead. How are you?"

"Can't complain." She backed out of his embrace and they both said in unison, "It wouldn't help anyway," then dissolved in laughter.

Private joke, Gabe thought, not altogether happy at how chummy the two appeared. Another reminder that he might have known Lindsey years ago, but they both lead different lives now. So what if she considered Mike a good friend? He was a good guy.

Through high school, Mike and Ty had been best buddies. As Ty's younger brother, Gabe knew Mike well enough, even if they hadn't hung with the same group of friends. Still, they'd had a good relationship, until right now, when the sudden male challenge for territory simmered between them. That territory being Lindsey.

As if just remembering Gabe was there, Lindsey turned to him, a smile curving her lips. "Come say hello to Mike."

Gabe joined them. "Good to see you again." He held out his hand and exchanged a hearty shake. "How long are you here for?"

"Indefinitely." Mike nodded at Gabe. "Heard you came back to town. Hanging around for a while?"

"For good."

"Gabe, so glad you could come," Laurel Ann greeted him without much pleasure in her voice.

"Mother, I think you should—"

"Lindsey, be a dear and bring the boys something to drink. Dinner will be ready soon."

Lindsey sent both men a questioning frown, glared at her mother and stomped off to the house.

"Play nice, boys," Laurel Ann purred as she sauntered away.

"What's that supposed to mean?" Mike asked.

"She has a plan." Gabe's wayward gaze followed Lindsey's shapely legs as she strode to the house. He sighed when she disappeared inside, then turned his attention back to Mike. "Unfortunately for you, she's made you part of it."

"Concerning Lindsey?" His brow furrowed and he ran a hand through burnished blond hair.

"She's got Lindsey on a major dating campaign. You're the next candidate."

"I think I missed something important here," Mike grumbled.

Despite his not wanting Mike getting involved with Lindsey, Gabe grinned. "You'd run for the hills if I told you what's been going on."

"Laurel Ann cornered me in the General Store earlier today, pressuring me to come out to this picnic. She rambled on about Lindsey needing my help, but came across very cryptic. Lindsey's a good friend, so I came out today to find out how I could help."

"I'm sure Laurel Ann counted on that."

Mike's eyes narrowed. "So then what are you doing with Lindsey?"

"We're friends. Lindsey needed a lift home from the library and Emily is here."

"Okay, so you're here. I'm here. What's next that I should know about?"

Gabe spied Lindsey hurrying toward them, tall glasses of sweet tea in each hand. "You'll have to ask Lindsey."

Lindsey handed them each a glass when she arrived. "What're you guys talking about?"

"How I'm out of the loop." Mike looked helplessly from Gabe to Lindsey.

Lindsey laughed. "I'm sorry, Mike. I think Mother may have nefarious plans for you."

"So I've heard."

She patted him on the shoulder like a he was a little boy. "Don't worry. I'll save you."

"You always do."

Once again Gabe frowned at the idea of Lindsey and Mike sharing a close relationship. And why should it bother him? He was still waiting to see where this thing with Lindsey would go, if he could get serious with a woman again.

She'd made what she wanted clear: love, and nothing less. He still had to deal with that and there was no telling how long Lindsey would wait for the right man.

And despite all his brilliant, lawyer-like arguments with himself, the bottom line was, he didn't like to see her with another guy. What did that say about his conflicting feelings for her?

Man, this whole thing gave him a headache.

Just as he thought it best to get Emily and head home, a white SUV pulled up the driveway and pulled off to park in the grass. Ty jumped out and hurried to the other side to help Casey out. They joined the group, smiling at the sight of Mike.

"Hey, buddy," Ty said as he pounded him on the back in greeting while Casey stepped into Mike's outstretched arms. "Hope you're hanging around for a while."

Casey stepped out of his embrace. "Maybe you can stay until the baby is born."

Mike's face softened as he gazed down at Casey. "Wouldn't miss it for the world."

"Great." Ty slipped his arm around Casey's shoulders. "Another male at my wife's beck and call."

"I can't help it if I get hungry and you won't let me drive to the grocery store." Casey patted her belly. "I am eating for two."

"And I'm running around for two," Ty joked.

"Just add me to the list, another willing gopher," Mike told her.

"Hey, while you're here, I need your help with something." Ty nodded to his wife. "You mind if we talk now?"

Casey waved him off, "No. Go ahead."

The two men walked away. Gabe shoved his hands into his slacks pockets, at a loss of what to do now.

"Lindsey, could I bother you for a drink?"

"Oh, gosh, sorry Casey. Sure, I'll get you some juice."

"Sounds wonderful." Casey turned to smile at Gabe once Lindsey headed to the house. "Since my husband has a pressing conversation to attend to, would you mind coming with me and sit for a while?"

"Anytime." He held out his arm and Casey took his gentlemanly offer to escort her to a grouping of chairs a short distance away.

"Some days I wonder how I'll last carrying around this weight, then I remember I still have a short time to go and can't imagine getting any bigger."

"You really look great, Casey. Happy. Content."

"Thanks. I needed to hear that."

"I remember how Cindy felt before Emily was born. A cross between elation and fearing the baby would never come. All I can tell you is, it's all worth it when you hold that baby in your arms for the first time."

Casey carefully lowered herself into a lawn chair. "Keep reminding me."

Gabe chuckled. "I can do that."

"Oh, what a beautiful way to end the day. I love springtime in the mountains. The flowers are blooming and the air is warm, even though I feel like a roasting oven." Casey closed her eyes and lifted her face to the waning sunshine. Gabe sat beside her, smiling at his sister-in-law's relaxed face. At times like this, he missed that connection to someone special. He wanted that again, but would he ever be up for the task? As Gran had reminded him, memories didn't give you comfort when you were lonely late at night.

Out of the corner of his eye he saw Lindsey approach and wondered again where this thing between them would lead. He wanted to spend all his spare time with her. Found himself thinking about her at the strangest times, which lately had multiplied to every minute of the day. He wanted to ask her opinion about things, wanted to just sit with her in the quiet, enjoying the intimate connection that had slipped into their friendship. And then in the next second, he wanted to kiss her senseless.

Then suddenly, a thought hit him right smack in the solar

plexus, leaving him gulping for air. Could he be in love with her?

Lindsey handed a glass of juice to Casey. His pulse kicked up a beat as he watched her, her unruly hair gleaming in the sun, the slight breeze ruffling the collar of her blouse, lifting the ends of her curly hair. Her natural beauty caught him off guard, like it had every day since the first time he saw her after returning home. Suddenly she didn't resemble the friend he'd teased on the way over here this afternoon. She'd morphed into a living, breathing dream-come-true—a total woman. A woman he'd kissed in the moonlight. A woman who made his pulse race. A woman, he decided, he wanted for his own.

Oh, man, he was definitely in love.

After handing the glass to Casey, Lindsey glanced at Gabe. Chills skittered down her spine. The wry smile and hooded expression resembled Emily's just before all heck broke loose.

Before she had a chance to question his mood, Dawn and Emily ran into the group. Emily hugged Casey, then pulled Dawn into that hug. As she watched the group hug, it hit her again, just as it had so many times these past few weeks. Dawn needed a real family, and Emily was slowly and methodically dragging Dawn into the Banner family. Where did that leave her?

She exchanged a puzzled glance with Gabe, wondering if he read the same scenario. And if he did, how would he handle it? She wasn't sure she wanted to know.

Daddy called out that dinner was ready, neatly drawing her from her thoughts. Ty and Mike had rejoined the group, Dorothea and Laurel Ann brought out the salads and everything else the large group needed.

Lindsey stood rooted to the spot, not sure, exactly, what she should do. Talk to Gabe? No, too awkward. Warn Mike about her mother's plans? No, the enjoyment on his face was too precious to ruin right before dinner. How had her life turned into such chaos in such a short time?

"Hey, you ready to eat?"

She blinked, then focused on Gabe standing beside her.

"I'm not very hungry." One thing was sure, if the turmoil in her life kept up, she'd lose some weight from her lack of appetite alone.

"Are you okay?"

"Sure. Let's go eat."

Lindsey filled a plate, but eventually picked at her food. Why, oh why, did Gabe have to be the only man for her? Why couldn't they have gotten together years ago, like she'd dreamed? If she could change the past, she'd let Gabe know *she* sent the note, not Cindy.

She set her jaw firmly. That wouldn't do her any good now. The past was the past, and she was too much of a pragmatist to wallow in what might have been. If Gabe didn't want to get serious, that was his problem. She still had to find a fake fiancé to make her sister keep her word.

Her gaze moved to Mike. He and Ty sat together, catching up on each other's lives. Pondering the possibilities, she gave Mike a thorough once over: Very handsome, and she knew his almost-bleached blond hair and dark tan were natural results of a man spending serious time outdoors. Tall, lean, and healthy. And when he flashed her his sweetest smile, she waited for her heart to react.

Nothing. She smiled back, not wanting to be rude, but her heart sank. They were good friends, nothing more. Nothing romantic here.

Even in high school, the issue of romance didn't come up between them. Their friendship started when they'd met in art class. Mike excelled, but Lindsey worked hard and always came up with miserable looking stick people.

Mike hated literature, so Lindsey helped him understand the beauty of books. They formed an easy friendship which had continued after graduation.

Over the years she'd run across his name in various publications as the art world took notice of his work. The first time she'd seen his work displayed, she'd been thrilled. But her genuine fondness for him was a far cry from love.

Currently he had a few pieces displayed at Crafty Creations in town, but while he was home she hoped to introduce Mike to Alanna, and schedule a date for a showing at the library.

She always had a blast with him, but to be honest, he didn't get under her skin the way Gabe did. He didn't make her hot one minute, crazy with longing the next. He simply hadn't grabbed hold of her heart strings and refused to let go. Only Gabe had been able to do that.

After dinner, as the loud and laughing group ate dessert, Lindsey went into the kitchen with a tray of condiments to put away. Her mind, heavy into scenarios to help her unwanted single situation, kept her from hearing Mike until he was right behind her.

"Hey, did you hear me?"

She nearly jumped five feet. "Jeez, Mike, you scared me."

"I made enough noise coming in."

She placed a hand over her diaphragm as she attempted to breath normally. "I'm sorry, my mind was elsewhere."

"Yeah, I noticed, right from about the time I got here today."

She laughed. "You always were the attentive one."

"Lindsey, you're acting weird. What's up?"

"I have to get engaged."

His eyebrows shot up. "What?"

"It's Risa. She's playing the custody card again. She's

found a guy and wants to get married, but also wants Dawn's future settled. Not that she wants to be a mother, but she's threatening to never give me custody unless I get married."

"I always thought she was nuts."

"Yeah, well, I believe her this time. She's serious."

"Which leaves you where?"

"Needing a fiance by the spring dance. You know, the library fundraiser."

Mike expelled a long breath as he leaned his hip against the counter. "Is that why Gabe's here?"

"No." She didn't want to tell Mike that Gabe had offered to help her out of this predicament, but that she couldn't accept. Because if she told him that, he'd know the depth of her feelings for Gabe, and she didn't want to argue the merits of having a family versus having a husband who truly loved her. "Gabe and I have spent some time together because of the girls."

He stared at her for a long drawn out moment. "There's more you're not telling me."

True, but she wasn't going to fill him in on her stressed emotional state right now. "My mother has been on the prowl for me. I've gone out on a few dates, but I can't make a decision as monumental as this with a man I barely know."

"You know me."

"Mike, I would never ask you to marry me because of my sister's demands." And it was true. She didn't love Mike. But she did love Gabe. As much as she went along with the dating thing, even when Gabe asked her out, she hoped that maybe Gabe would want to marry her. The other guys might have been a way to appease her sister, but with Gabe, well, her heart was lost to him. She didn't get that same spark of excitement with Mike or any other man. The fake dates had proven that Gabe was the only man for her.

"Besides, Mike, marriage, in our case, would ruin a beautiful friendship."

He flashed a crooked smile. "No fireworks, hmm?"

"Sorry. And you can't say you're pining away for me."

"True enough." His expression sobered. "You know I'd do anything for you. Besides, I'm not involved in a relationship right now. Maybe we can fake out your sister long enough to make her happy."

"Yeah, and what happens if you find the perfect woman between now and then?"

"I doubt that'll happen."

"You never know, Mike."

He ran his hand through his hair. "So what are you going to do?"

Her shoulders slumped. "I don't know."

Mike closed the distance between them and hugged her. It felt good to have strong arms around her, they just belonged to the wrong man.

"Promise me you won't hesitate to ask if you need me."

She pulled away. "I would never put you in the situation of settling, Mike. That's what it would be with us. We both deserve more than settling for second place to satisfy my sister."

He nodded. "So, you're sure you and Gabe can't give it a try? I know you've always had a thing for him."

"He's not ready." It hurt just to admit it.

"You've talked about it?"

"A little."

"Wow. From what Ty tells me, he doesn't discuss his private life with anyone, at least beyond his family."

"We go back a long way. I'm sure he feels comfortable with me."

"Then he's the crazy one."

She arched an eyebrow. "Why?"

"To have a chance with you and blow it? He needs some serious sense knocked into him."

"Well, you will *not* be doing any knocking, got that?"

He saluted her. "Yes, Miss Schoolteacher."

She laughed, at his response. He really thought she had a chance with Gabe? That she was worth Gabe's attention? This sure gave her something to think about. In the meantime, Mike's teasing and good humor lessened the impact of the situation.

Ty walked in as they were laughing, his eyes narrowing. "Hey, what's going on in here?" He singled out Lindsey with his laser gaze.

"Mike and I started talking and the time flew away. Did you need something, Ty?"

He grinned. "Got any ice cream?"

Lindsey crossed the room and opened the freezer to peer inside. "Casey's having cravings again?"

"Big time."

She grabbed a carton of Rocky Road she knew Casey would enjoy, then added a spoon and handed it to Ty. "Go, Dad, before she changes her mind and requests pickles."

Mike left with Ty and Lindsey went back to the task of cleaning up her grandmother's kitchen.

"Need any help?"

Startled, Lindsey glanced up from loading the dishwasher. Gabe stood in the doorway, his sheer male presence filling the room as he leaned against the doorjamb in a lazy, relaxed pose. The setting sun behind him bathed him in a golden glow.

She swallowed hard, trying to hide the pleasure she felt at his presence. "No, just putting away a few dishes. Thanks anyway."

"The girls are out running around, but I wanted to thank you for today before I took Emily home."

"You're leaving so early?"

"Yeah, Em and I haven't spent too much time together lately. I thought we'd hang out, maybe catch up on her math homework."

On a Saturday night? Lindsey's worst suspicions rose and settled heavily in her heart. She covered her shaky hands by grabbing the dishcloth. "Before you leave, I need to talk to you."

Gabe's eyes grew shuttered. "Shoot."

When he didn't move from his position in the doorway, Lindsey took a deep breath and asked, "Gabe, no matter what happens between you and me, you won't keep Emily from hanging around with Dawn, will you?"

He frowned. "Of course not, but where is this coming from?"

"My sister has made my life very complicated right now." She began to pace the confines of the kitchen, hoping words wouldn't fail her now. "However things go, I'd like the girls to remain friends."

He dropped his arms and shoved his hands in his pants pockets. "Ah, I see. I don't want commitment and you might find the right man, is that it?

So glad that he understood, she waved her hand, the dishcloth arching in the air with her motion. "It may or may not happen, but, I mean, we wouldn't stop being friends, we just couldn't hang out or do anything together. I'm sure you'd agree. If you found a woman you wanted to get involved with, you wouldn't want to be spending time with me."

"It won't happen because I'm not looking. And besides, aren't you rushing things just a bit?"

Yes. I only have a few weeks.

"I'm thinking ahead, Gabe."

He didn't look pleased and his tone told her so. "I would never keep them apart, Lindsey, no matter what you and I do or don't do. You're making this difficult."

"That's because I'm in a difficult spot."

"Then get out of it."

"Oh, you should talk. You want a family for Emily, and you'd be willing to marry a woman you didn't love to give her that security. We're not much different."

"What do you mean?" he asked quietly.

"What I mean is that Dawn is everything to me and I'll do what I have to do for her."

Chapter Eleven

Dawn and Emily ran as far as they could through the dense woods before stopping to catch their breath.

"You heard them. They wouldn't keep us apart, would they?" Dawn bent over after asking the question, her arms hugging her aching stomach.

"Not if I can help it," Emily yanked at a twig caught in her hair. "Once Daddy gets an idea in his head, it's hard for him to change his mind."

Taking a deep breath, Dawn sat on a nearby stump. Emily sank down beside her and asked, "How far do you think we ran?"

"Not far enough. We have to keep going so when they miss us, we won't be that easy to find."

Emily scratched her calf. "It's better than sitting around and letting them make the decisions."

"They are the adults."

Emily gazed up at her friend. "I know, but when we wanted to get them together, I thought it would be easy. I know it's hard for Dad, I miss Mom too, but even I know we have to keep going on. Mom's not coming back."

Blinking back tears, Dawn stared at her friend. "I might have my mom, Risa, but she doesn't feel real. Lindsey has always been there for me, while my real mom goes off to wherever she wants. It's not fair, not for either of us." She sniffled. "I don't understand. We can see that your dad and Lindsey should get together, why can't they?"

Silence settled over their still forms until Emily spoke again. "They need our help, Dawn."

"But we tried."

"Is there any place around here we can hide out?"

"Let me think." Dawn closed her eyes, going over the property surrounding them, trying to figure out where they could go. "I remember hiking near here with Granddaddy Ed. There was a hollow we stopped in, it had a small waterfall. If I can find the right path, maybe we could hang out there for a while."

Emily stared into the dense woods. "It'll be dark really soon."

"Do you want to go back?"

She shrugged, as if she didn't care, but her shoulders were stiff. "I don't know."

"Let's try for the hollow. If we don't find it, we can head back home."

Emily grinned, mischief in her eyes, even in the dire situation. "Maybe if our folks have to search for us, they'll get closer."

"That's a good plan. They can worry about us together."

"Yeah, and adults love to do that stuff." Standing, Emily brushed dried leaves and dirt from the seat of her shorts. "You're sure you know where you're going?"

Dawn glanced over at her bold friend, surprised by the hesitancy in her voice. Suddenly, Emily didn't look too sure about this hike into the woods. "We'll be fine. Although, Granddaddy Ed probably knows every hideout in the woods. I don't know if we could fool him."

"We have to try," she waved off Dawn's concern with forced bravado. "Besides, they'll probably find us before it's time to go to bed."

Together they headed into the darkening shadows, Dawn taking the lead for the first time in their friendship while she repeated over and over in her mind that things would be fine. They had to be, didn't they?

Gabe rounded the corner of the house, Lindsey's parting words still echoing in his head. What was she thinking? With the mutinous look on her face when she left the kitchen, he hadn't asked her to be specific.

Her sister's demands were wearing on her. Besides the fact that Lindsey really wanted a family, deep in his gut he couldn't believe she'd marry a man she didn't love.

He knew Lindsey enough to know that love motivated her actions. Her love for Dawn and family. But their conversation in the kitchen concerned him. Could her sister have changed the plan and he didn't know about it? It would explain why Lindsey warned him that she might find someone else to make the dating plan work.

Still, the thought of Lindsey with another guy made him crazy inside. He knew it was unfair to have this unbridled, protective side especially when he didn't offer her what she seemed to want, himself. Shoot, he was just getting used to the idea of loving again.

He ran his hand over his face, cringing at his selfish need to keep Lindsey all to himself. He couldn't picture his life without her in it. Not meeting up with her like they did now, to spend time talking and laughing. They were so natural together, as if the years apart had melted away to yesterday.

The fact that he'd been married didn't seem to be an issue for Lindsey. She understood what he'd had with Cindy, respected it even. Wanted it for herself.

He hadn't really helped matters, he realized. His off-handed proposal didn't come anywhere near what Lindsey would have dreamed of. He'd seen the hurt in her eyes. And now that he realized he loved her, he understood how she felt. Yet she wouldn't be deterred from her goal. As much as he admired that trait, it also drove him to distraction.

He could argue with Lindsey about her decision until he was hoarse, but the fact of the matter was, he wasn't any better at handling this attraction between them than she was. Being alone with Lindsey sent him reeling. Her scent made him lightheaded, and when he managed to touch her soft skin, well, desires he hadn't felt in a long time overwhelmed him. He felt like a teen all over again, with the crazy swing of emotions and the excitement mixed with anxiety when he knew he was going to see her. So much for the suave, debonair man of the world he wanted to project. Their disaster of a conversation in the kitchen confirmed that.

The sound of laughter pulled him from his depressing thoughts. Might as well get Emily and head on home. He was definitely finished here tonight.

He approached the crowd playing cards at the picnic table and asked, "Anyone seen the girls?"

Laurel Ann pointed in the direction of Lindsey's cottage. "I thought I saw them run off just a bit ago. Check that way."

"Thanks."

He tried not to look like he was in an all-fire hurry to get away from the Summer compound, no matter how true. He needed some time to think about his quarrel with Lindsey, then find a way to fix it. He'd come up with a viable solution they could all live with. He may not have had a happy ending in his marriage to Cindy, but he sure could do something about this crazy, mixed-up notion Lindsey had of marrying the first guy who came along.

"Emily!" he called out as he neared the cottage. The only response came from crickets beginning their evening serenade as the sun set. "Dawn?"

He circled the house, not catching any glimpses of the girls, nor hearing any tell-tale giggles or shushing that would give away their hiding place.

The fine hairs on the back of his neck bristled in warning. Gabe turned, heading back the way he came.

Lindsey came around the side of her grandmother's house just as he returned.

"Have you seen the girls? It's getting dark and I want to be sure Em is okay."

"No. I was just looking for them myself. They always like to play hide-and-seek when it's time to go home, but they've never gone this long."

"I checked around your house. There's no sign of them."

"Did you try the barn?"

"No. Let's go."

He took Lindsey's hand and jogged to the darkened barn looming beside the fringes of the woods. He doubted Emily would be in that structure. She didn't like to be in the dark, never had, even as a small child.

The wood door squeaked as he opened it and stepped into the dusty opening. Beside him, Lindsey peered in. "Emily, are you in here?"

The silence was deafening. He backed out and squinted into the murky shadows enveloping the woods behind the barn. "They wouldn't have walked into the dark woods at this late hour, would they?"

"I thought maybe they were playing with us, but now I'm not so sure."

"I'm getting a bad feeling about this, Linds. Emily wouldn't hide out in the dark, even to stretch out her time here tonight."

Lindsey grimaced, the seriousness of his concern about Emily obviously spooking her. "Let's go to Gramma's house and see if they're watching TV."

Gabe took the front steps two at a time, throwing open the front door, all the time praying the girls were inside, laying on the floor in front of the television. One lamp glowed in the far corner of the cluttered room, shedding enough light for him to view an empty room. The TV cast an eerie glow on the barren floor in front of it.

He went from room to vacant room calling their names. Fear uncoiled in his stomach. He joined Lindsey in the living room. "They aren't there."

"Something is seriously wrong." Concern shadowed Lindsey's eyes. "Let's ask the others for help."

With her hand entwined with his, Gabe led them to the picnic table. The conversation, which appeared to debate the merits of which kind of mayonnaise, Blue Ribbon or Hellmans, was the best to use on a tomato and mayo sandwich, served on white bread, of course, came to an abrupt halt. Gabe launched right into telling them his concerns.

"The girls are gone. We've been calling and we can't find them. We checked the houses and the barn. Nothing."

Granddaddy Ed rose quickly for his advanced years. "I got some lanterns in my shed. I'll fetch them."

"Let's search in pairs," said Lindsey's father, who stood, helping Laurel Ann beside him, "that way we won't be scattered about when we find them. I have two-way radios if we need them, but for now, let's work the perimeter of the property and meet back here in fifteen minutes."

"Don't panic before we know what's really happening," Dorothea cautioned them all.

Lindsey automatically followed Gabe. His tense shoulders and purposeful stride indicated he was just as worried, although he'd kept his words calm. No doubt that demeanor had made him the successful lawyer he was.

"Hold up," she called.

He slowed his pace until she reached his side, then she had to adjust her steps to keep up with him. "This has to be a mistake. Why would the girls go off into the woods this late in the day?"

"I'm hoping it's like you said, they're playing a game."

She didn't like his tone. "What else could it be?"

He didn't answer, leaving Lindsey to dwell on the question at hand. Obviously he didn't want to think the worst any more than she did.

What were the girls thinking?

They called out into the darkness, getting no answer in return. Lindsey glanced at her watch, amazed that another fifteen minutes had gone by so quickly. She touched Gabe's rigid arm. "Let's head back to the others. If they didn't find the girls, we'll form plan B."

Gabe scanned the woods intensely before his troubled gaze met hers. He nodded.

"We'll come back and search, but we need the others, Gabe."

He looked hesitant about stopping the search, even for a few minutes to regroup, and with one last long look into the darkness, he took her hand and retraced their steps.

Two hours later, the sheriff had arrived with local volunteers, all out searching. Ty went to get Ruby Sue, worried about what the news of her beloved Emily out in the woods at night might do to her health. She rallied, manning the phone, calling everyone in town to find out if they knew anything. Dorothea and Laurel Ann kept the coffee coming.

The family had been asked to stay together and not wander off and impede the search. Of course, Granddaddy Ed had disappeared, but that didn't surprise Lindsey. In fact, it gave her a small measure of comfort. If anyone knew the land well enough to find the girls, it was Granddaddy.

Gabe had been in the forefront of the search, with Lindsey by his side, but they'd come back for a progress report. Some distance away from the crowd he took up his post beside a tall oak. His face conveyed the worry he'd been battling. She knew, because she felt the same way. Her heart ached and she needed to touch him right then and have him assure her that this nightmare would be over quickly.

She walked up to him, taking his warm hand in hers, and said quietly, "This is my fault. I should have taken you seriously when you thought the girls were missing."

He pulled her into his embrace, reassuring her with his body as well as his words. "Don't worry about that. You didn't know."

She fell into his arms, ignoring the rise of tears behind her lids. "Maybe we would have found them if I'd listened to you."

"Don't second guess yourself, Linds." He tightened his hold on her and she gladly circled her arms around his waist. The warmth of his hard body against her cheek brought much needed comfort.

"They've got to be okay," she whispered against his shoulder.

Gabe tried to speak, coughed away his emotion, then spoke. "I can't lose Em too."

At his softly spoken, heartfelt words, Lindsey's heart

broke. She thought about Gabe loosing Cindy and maybe Emily, and she held him closer.

"I knew something was up, I felt it," he said with a quiet rasp.

Why hadn't she felt that Dawn was missing or up to something? Had she been too wrapped up in her own conflict of emotions with Gabe? She'd been so worried about a future without him, and now, with the girls missing, her problems seemed meager in contrast. She shivered. How could she not sense that Dawn was in danger?

"Hey," Gabe pulled back and peered into her eyes. "I know what you're doing. Don't beat yourself up."

"I keep telling myself that the girls aren't going anywhere. That in a minute, they'll be back with us."

Gabe idly played with a strand of her hair then took a deep breath and loosened his hold of her. "We need to keep looking."

Lindsey nodded and stepped back while wiping her damp cheeks. As much as she longed for Gabe's strong arms around her, assuring and comforting her, she agreed with the need to keep searching. "You're right."

They set off on another path, their flashlight beams bobbing as they walked. Finally Lindsey voiced a thought that had been haunting her all night. "Do you think they might have overheard us talking in the kitchen?"

"I think it's a good possibility."

"But why would they disappear?"

"In case you haven't noticed, they've been playing matchmaker with us."

"Yes, I noticed."

"I have no doubt that Emily came up with this idea. But this goes far beyond a game. I don't think she considered the darkness. Or the consequences."

Lindsey shuddered. "I've been praying, Gabe. They'll be fine, no matter their reasons for taking off. I think God especially protects kids who act before they think."

"That's Em," he said in a gruff half-whisper. "And thanks for the prayers."

Lindsey took a deep breath and closed her eyes. In the distance she heard the squawk of a walkie-talkie and the low murmurs of the folks gathered together, keeping each other's spirits up.

Through the brush, Lindsey spotted a car slowly moving down the driveway, and for a panicked second, she hoped it wouldn't be Risa. It turned out to be a search volunteer, but Lindsey couldn't help but wonder what would happen when her sister found out about Dawn's disappearance. She swallowed heavily. If Risa wanted, she could take Dawn away, regardless of the demands she'd put on Lindsey, even if Lindsey did carry out her plan.

By one o'clock in the morning, Lindsey's nerves were shot. She and Gabe had returned to the central command waiting to find out where they'd search next. Suddenly a shout sounded from behind the barn. Lindsey stared up at Gabe, and their gazes connected for mere seconds before they both took off running toward the sound.

The entire family followed, just as Granddaddy Ed came from the woods with two bow-headed girls in tow.

Gabe ran toward Emily, scooping her into his arms as Lindsey followed suit with Dawn. Both girls looked sleepy and contrite, but physically fine. Lindsey didn't care. She kept running her hands over Dawn, making sure she was in one piece, no broken bones or injuries.

"It's okay, really," Dawn protested over Lindsey's fussing. "We're fine."

"Yeah, Dad," Emily chimed in. "We're okay."

Granddaddy joined the group, a half-grin relaxing his

tired features. "Have to say, the girls found themselves a good hiding spot. If I hadn't had a feeling they were nearby, I mighta missed them."

The collective group moved from the barn to the clearing by Gramma's house, amidst tears and smiles of relief and happiness. Lindsey wouldn't give up her hold on Dawn until she realized the other family members needed to hold her too. The girls moved from one family member to the next, while she and Gabe stood back and watched.

"They are in *so* much trouble," Gabe said just above a whisper for her ears only.

Before long, they thanked the law enforcement officers and volunteers as they headed home after a late night. The family stared to disperse. Dawn and Emily came over for another long hug. Lindsey breathed in Dawn's scent and sent another prayer of thanks. She reached out to ruffle Emily's hair before embracing her as well.

Over the girls' heads, Lindsey met Gabe's gaze. Although visibly relaxed now, she could still see the remnants of fear in his eyes. And she remembered what he'd said about the girls' motive for running away, to get their attention. Now, more than ever, deep in her soul, Lindsey understood how much these girls needed a mother and a father. How much they needed to be a family.

She nodded to Gabe with a tired smile and whispered, "Yes."

He raised a brow in question.

Then she mouthed the words, "Yes, I'll marry you."

Chapter Twelve

The three weeks following the girls' safe return flew by in a whirlwind for Lindsey. The girls were over the moon about the engagement. Risa drove out to the house, not upset about the night of the runaway, full of hugs and thanks and unsolicited advice. Lindsey bit the inside of her cheek to keep from making any inflammatory remarks. She'd reached the goal of being engaged by tomorrow night's gala and her sister was happy. She'd leave it like that for now.

Her grandparents were happy, and even skeptical Laurel Ann slowly came around to the idea. All was right with the world. Lindsey should be happy, right?

But she wasn't. In the midst of her dream becoming reality, she couldn't shake the nagging melancholy that their upcoming wedding was far from real. Gabe, for the most part, acted like this whole engagement thing was what he wanted, but deep down, Lindsey knew he did it as a favor to her and, after the girls' stunt, to give them stability. She knew it was nothing more. After all, Gabe hadn't said he loved her.

And she hadn't told him she couldn't have children.

She stood by her bedroom window, staring out at the profusion of color in the richly blooming flowers under the bright spring sun, her mood dark and heavy. She knew it had to do with her reluctance to turn around and uncover the two new dresses that lay on her bed.

Her thoughts went back to the gala. The dress for the library fundraiser had caught her eye the last time she went to a small boutique she loved in Gainesville. An original, the gown had a sleeveless bodice with multicolored beads lavishly adorning the black fabric. The long flowing georgette skirt of basic black slenderized her curves, and with the strappy black sandals, made her appear tall and slim.

A slight smile curved on her lips as she remembered trying the outfit on in the trendy boutique. Back then, she never in a million years would have imagined the turn of events for the night she actually wore the dress. At the time, she only knew she liked it and wanted to make a splash at the dance.

After the night Lindsey had agreed to marry Gabe, he asked to be her escort to the gala. She was thrilled, and a bit nervous. Especially when he suggested they use the fundraiser gathering as a formal way to announce the engagement and set a date. Okay, she could deal with that for now, but the wedding itself? Suddenly the actions of the past few weeks became all to real.

Shaking her head, she walked to the bed and gently removed the black gown and hanger from the protective bag. Tomorrow night would be here much too soon. She hung it over the closet door, standing back to admire the simplicity, yet the intricate working of the beads.

This is a lot like my life.

She crossed her arms over her chest and turned to stare at the other, bigger bag. Inside lay her dream wedding dress. She'd shown her mother a picture of the gown she'd cut out of *Bride* magazine years ago. This morning, Laurel Ann personally delivered it to her door. Her mother had ordered it on the sly through her connections in the fashion world, as a surprise for Lindsey. Boy, what a surprise. The reality of the dress made the reality of a wedding much more, well, real.

Lindsey tentatively fingered the plastic covering before pulling down the zipper to reveal the dress. She carefully removed it from the bag to hang it from the back of her bedroom door, then took a step back.

Simple, yet undeniably elegant. A gorgeous white confection of a fitted bodice covered in luminescent seed pearls with off-the-shoulder sleeves, and yards and yards of soft chiffon to glide around her. The detachable, mid-length train carried a detailed floral design, also done in the pearls, that would glitter as she walked down the isle on Daddy's arm.

As she admired the dress, she glimpsed a tag inside the neckline. Reaching out to remove it, a hidden pin jabbed her finger. Jerking her hand back as if the dress had suddenly starting shooting sparks, Lindsey panicked. She grabbed her purse and briefcase, then rushed out of the room. As it was, she was already running late for school. Fridays were always hectic and she hoped the inquisitive children and the ultimately busy day would clear the worries and distractions that fogged her mind.

She was doing the right thing by getting married, she firmly assured herself. For Dawn, Emily and Gabe.

Wasn't she?

Later that evening, Lindsey sat curled up in a library chair when Alanna appeared and flopped down in the empty chair beside her. "It's almost six o'clock. Closing time."

"Already?"

"Yeah. You've been lost in that book for over two hours now. Care to tell me what's up?"

"To be honest, I needed some down time with a good book so I wouldn't think about the current events that have become my life."

"I guess that explains why you're hiding in the farthest back corner of the building, reading." She leaned down to read the name on the spine of the book, "*The Great Escape*?"

Lindsey grimaced.

"Okay, we have something very Freudian going on here. What's up?"

Lindsey closed the book and placed it on the nearby table. She had yet to verbalize to anyone her confused state of mind.

Her petite friend sat nestled in her seat, expecting answers.

"Would you believe me if I told you I'm nervous about the wedding preparations and wanted to mentally escape for a few hours?"

"No, I wouldn't believe you. It's me, the friend you stayed here with late one night when we got talking about the perfect wedding scenarios. The night the sheriff showed up because the lights were still burning in the library and it was way after closing hours. Remember that night, because I do. I can still—"

Lindsay held up her hand. "Okay, okay, I get the message. You're not buying my excuse."

"No, I'm not."

"Well, there's Mom to deal with. She'll probably change everything to suit herself, anyway."

"You already have a default plan for that."

"Oh, yeah. You're right." She ran a hand over her denim skirt to smooth the wrinkles before fiddling with the bottom button of her blouse. "We haven't formally announced the engagement . . ."

"So, what's really bothering you?"

"I realize I have to do this for Dawn. And everything is happening so fast, but—"

"But?"

"But it makes me realize how bad I want this to be real. To have a long engagement, to really enjoy all the romance around this whole matrimony thing. I never dreamed it would end up like this, especially with Gabe."

Alanna grew silent for long moments, as if she were weighing Lindsey's words. "So," she ventured, "are you having second thoughts about ending the engagement?"

"No. No. I'm not. With all the dating, and planning the fundraiser, and dealing with the girls' disappearance, I guess I'm just overwhelmed." She took a deep breath and continued, mainly to convince herself. "I can deal with this engagement."

"You're not supposed to deal with it, you're supposed to enjoy it."

Lindsey grinned at her serious friend. "How do you know?"

"Because I was engaged once, a long time ago."

A flash of pain, so fleeting, passed over Alanna's face.

"I suppose there's a story in this somewhere."

"Yes, but you're depressed enough for one day."

"That doesn't sound good."

"We're talking about you."

"Seems like we're always talking about mc," Lindsey muttered.

Alanna brushed off her seriousness with a grin. "You *are* the one engaged."

Lindsey glanced down at her ringless finger. Somehow that seemed appropriate. "Yep, I am."

"Then quit moping and get busy. It's too beautiful a day to be holed up in here. If you must read, at least go to the park for a little while until the sun sets."

That's what she needed, fresh air to clear her mind. Lindsey stood up and gathered her belongings. "Thanks, Alanna. Really."

"Just keep a bridesmaid space open for me and we'll call it even."

Lindsey's heart sank. "I'll do that."

Gabe drove around the park a second time to make sure the woman sitting on the park bench was Lindsey. Really, he had no doubt it was her, he was procrastinating. He needed to talk to her, to confess that he'd fallen in love with her. He'd had plenty of time to think about it and realize that he did, indeed, love her to distraction. He was ready to confidently step into the future. And that meant telling Lindsey exactly what was in his heart.

Things between them had grown awkward since she agreed to marry him. She made excuses not to get together. She had her father bring Dawn over to visit Emily. It was like she was avoiding him. Not normal behavior for an engaged couple.

He thought maybe she regretted her decision made in the height of emotional turmoil. He, on the other hand, was ecstatic about her decision. She had inadvertently solidified his decision to move on with his life, make a real family with the girls, and hopefully add more children to the mix.

He had planned to steadily work her defenses down with

his considerable charm and wit and convince her to marry him. He laughed. Charm and wit had nothing to do with her answer. Two strong-willed girls turned the tide for him. Which made punishing Emily difficult.

Still, Lindsey's change of mood concerned and bothered him. Could she be having second thoughts? Only one way to find out, he had to ask. Then tell her that he'd fallen in love with her. Which he intended to do. Today. Now.

He parked and within minutes joined her on the bench.

"Hey, pretty lady," he said as he slid beside her.

"Hey, yourself," she answered, her eyes wide with surprise.

"I called the house. Dawn said she thought you were at the library."

"I was, then I walked over here. I needed a little time to myself."

"Worried about the gala?"

She nodded. "I hope it comes off without a hitch."

"With you in charge, it'll be great."

She warily glanced at him. "What're you doing here? I figured you'd be home now after spending a day with Ty working on the Olsen house renovations."

"We were, but Casey started with those contractions again, so Ty headed home and I decided to call it a day. I've been trying to track you down. I wanted to talk to you."

Her eyes clouded and she moved slightly away from him. "About . . . ?"

Where did he start? At the beginning, he supposed.

"Lindsey, do you really want to get married?"

Her eyes widened in surprise. "Why would you ask me that?"

"You've been acting funny lately. I wondered if you're

having second thoughts. I know we haven't exactly had the most traditional engagement."

"I'll admit, I've had a lot on my mind lately. Between Risa, the gala, thinking about wedding preparations—"

"I know Risa has made things tough on you. We can slow things down if you want."

"It's not Risa. In fact, she's like my long lost buddy these days."

"There must be something else."

"Actually, I've been sitting here, thinking about Cindy."

"Cindy?" Gabe stared at her. "Why?"

"I don't know. Being here in the park, I guess."

Gabe gazed around him, basking in the familiarity of the town park. A merry shriek grabbed his attention. A half dozen children dashed around the playground, climbing up the steps to the slide and laughing without a care in the world as they recklessly careened down from great heights to stop at the dirt spot at the bottom. A group of mothers stood guard nearby, most likely gossiping about their day. It reminded him of another day he'd been here, an important milestone in his life.

"Did you know this is the same bench I met Cindy at all those years ago?"

"Yes. At three-thirty, after school on a Friday afternoon, October twenty-fifth."

He gaped at her. "She showed you the note?"

Lindsey stared out over the park. "I wrote the note," she whispered.

"What?" Surely he hadn't heard her right. Cindy had always been rather secretive about their meeting. She never mentioned that she showed the note to anyone, but that didn't mean she hadn't, "Cindy never told me that."

"I'm sure she wouldn't have. You see, I wanted to meet you here. Cindy beat me to it."

Confusion rattled him. "What do you mean?"

"I wrote the note and told Cindy about it. She was my best friend and I was a little nervous and needed moral support. She took it from me, said she'd deliver it to you, and went down the hallway to her next class." A sad smile curved her lips. "Oh, she did change the time. I had originally wanted to meet at four o'clock. Anyway, I showed up and here you two sat. You know the rest of the story."

Gabe struggled to take a breath. "Why didn't you say anything?"

Lindsey's laugh sounded hoarse. "Why would I have? You both were extremely happy. I figured it was meant to be and went on with my life."

He shook his head. "I always wondered why you and Cindy didn't hang out much after that. I asked, but she only gave me a vague story."

"It's not a big deal, Gabe. She got the guy. End of story."

"It's not the end of the story. She lied to me. Our whole relationship was built on a lie."

"Wait a minute, don't let the actions of a teenager shake up your idea of the past. She loved you."

"She still lied to me."

"Gabe, I didn't tell you this to undermine your marriage."

"Then why did you?"

"I . . ." She stared up at him, wounded eyes dark with worry. "I'm not sure. I guess I wanted you to know that I've always loved you."

His chest ached around the vicinity of his heart. It was bad enough that something had been lacking in their marriage at the time Cindy died. Now, to learn this. And to discover that Lindsey had always loved him, yet sacrificed her feelings so he could be happy.

That note had changed the direction of his life. He'd

married young, had a daughter before finishing law school. He didn't regret those things, how could he? But still, the gravity of Cindy's actions hit him solidly in the chest. Taking a deep breath, he ran his hand through his hair.

"You know what's so ironic about this? I was going to ask you to the prom, but I got the note . . ."

"And I never went," Lindsey whispered, more to herself to Gabe.

After long taut seconds, Gabe stood. "I should get home."

"Gabe," Lindsey said as she grabbed hold of his hand. "Please don't be angry with me or Cindy. I'm sorry, I should have kept my mouth shut."

"No, it's okay. I needed to know the truth."

"It doesn't change things."

"You're right."

He studied her anguished expression and knew deep in his heart that she hadn't told him to purposely destroy him. If anything, he knew she didn't have a malicious bone in her body. Still, his past, present and future suddenly collided in a way that would forever change him. When he saw the tears in Lindsey's eyes, he knew she'd realized the same thing.

"I need time to think."

"Okay. Call me if you need to talk."

"Right. I'll see you tomorrow night."

He strode back to the Lexus, not seeing a thing other than the path before him. His ears buzzed and he felt nauseous. The car started smoothly, so unlike his life he thought with dark humor. As he pulled away he glimpsed Lindsey standing in the spot where he left her. She watched him drive away, gripping the back of the bench, the evening dusk silhouetting her shoulders, heavy with defeat.

He was halfway home before he realized he hadn't done the thing he set out to do—tell Lindsey he loved her.

Chapter Thirteen

The next evening, Gabe stood before the mirror in his room at Ruby Sue's house, tying his bow tie to finish dressing for the gala when a knock sounded on the door. "Come in."

Ruby Sue, dressed in a gown a muted shade of lavender, pushed into the room. "Still brooding?"

"That's Ty's job."

"Well, you're doin' a darned good imitation."

"Not now, Gran."

"Then when? When you meet Lindsey at the church altar with a frown on your face? That ain't a good way to start a marriage."

He let out a breath and ran a hand through his hair. "I don't know how I feel about marriage right now."

Ruby Sue sat on the bed and crossed her arms, making it clear she wasn't going anywhere. "Care to explain yourself?"

"I found out something about Cindy and our marriage." He told his grandmother the details of his conversation with Lindsey.

"So now you've decided that the institution of marriage isn't worth having because of what a teenage girl did to you?"

"What would you have me think?"

"That Cindy was ingenious in getting the man she wanted. She was young. You both were." Ruby Sue let out a pent-up breath. "Gabe, Lindsey knows you're helping her out by marrying her. Probably wishes for a lot more. But she loves you enough that she laid her concerns on the line by telling you what happened all those years ago."

"By telling me about the note, Lindsey was expressing her concerns? How do you figure that?"

"The girl has it bad for you. Always has. Now she's going to marry you, it's her dream come true. But look what's been happening around her. Her crazy sister's demand. Then the girls pull their little stunt. Her mamma settin' her up with any single guy in these parts. Lindsey's gotta wonder if you're marrying her because it's best for the girls, or if you really love her."

Gabe stared at his reflection in the mirror. Guilt nagged at him. "I haven't told her."

"Because it isn't true?"

"No. After learning about Cindy's secret and Lindsey keeping that secret, it makes me more wary than ever."

"That's just plain dumb."

He couldn't hold back his grin. "I can always count on you to speak your mind."

"Think about it, Gabe. Lindsey must be feeling awfully insecure."

His grandmother was right, but he'd never admit it to her.

"You know how much telling the truth means to me, Gran. If there's no trust, what do you have?"

"Nobody's perfect, boy, you should know that from

bein' a lawyer. People make mistakes. Maybe Lindsey should have told you the truth way back then, but she didn't. You gonna make her pay for it now? Think about how she felt, steppin' aside so you could be happy. So you see, she never betrayed your trust. If anything, she's tryin' to set out with a clean slate for your future. So here's my question to you. Does the past really matter that much, Gabe?"

Did it? In light of the future he would enjoy with Lindsey if he could just get his act together? God was giving him a chance to start again. He'd always have Cindy in his heart, but Lindsey had shown him that his heart was big enough to love her as well. That maybe, if he gave them a chance, their precious love would fully enrich his life in a way that was pure Lindsey, full of love and laughter.

"I suppose what happened in the past doesn't matter now, especially if I have Lindsey in my future." He had to put the past behind him for good. He realized that now.

Ruby Sue grinned. "That's my boy. I knew you'd figure it out."

Yeah, but leaving Lindsey alone, without confirmation of a future together, or telling her he loved her, probably sabotaged the wedding.

Lindsey frowned at herself in her bedroom mirror. Was she intentionally sabotaging this wedding? After she'd dreamed about it only . . . forever?

To bring up the note, what was wrong with her? Just trying to be honest, her inner voice taunted. Yeah, right. If she was really honest with herself, she'd admit that deep down inside, it bothered her that Gabe wouldn't give her his heart, even after she told him she loved him. Really, if she didn't have his heart, what kind of future could they have in name only? Oh, Dawn and Emily would be happy, but what about Gabe? And to remind him of the past? That was a story Gabe didn't need to hear. One look at his stricken face told her she'd blundered big time.

And what about the fact that she couldn't have children? Didn't Gabe deserve to know the truth? If she really wanted to be honest with herself, she'd admit that telling Gabe scared her more than anything else.

She shook her head. Pick yourself up, girl. The gala is tonight and you have to show, date or no date. The mayor expected her to be there—he'd told her earlier today that he had a message from the governor. It had to be about her literacy program. She should be excited, still . . .

Gabe hadn't called. He'd told her he'd see her tonight, but in light of the note conversation, she didn't really expect him to show. They had planned on bringing the girls to the dance for a short while, then have Granddaddy Ed and Gramma bring them back home when it got late. So really, there was no problem, she'd expected to go to the gala with Dawn from the early planning stages.

She let out a sigh and concentrated on dressing. At least her mother hadn't threatened her with a makeover before the dance. Lindsey pulled her hair back into a tasteful chignon and carefully applied her own makeup. Stepping back to view herself, Lindsey smiled. Laurel Ann would be proud when she saw her later this evening.

She carefully slipped the beaded top over her hair and then stepped into the full black skirt. She turned in a circle, watching the georgette swirl out around her. When she faced the mirror again, she stopped still. Who was this woman? Certainly not the same girl who'd looked at herself just a few weeks earlier. Now she stood here an engaged woman. At least, she thought she was still engaged. She'd have to see if Gabe changed his mind.

Rummaging around in her jewelry box, Lindsey found

the perfect pair of earrings to go with her dress. She had just finished with the final touches when her sister sauntered into the bedroom, looking every bit like a high-dollar fashion model.

"So, what do you think?" Risa asked. "Too overdone for this little hamlet?"

"As usual, you're spectacular."

"Good. It's been a long time since I've been to a social function in Paineville."

"Everyone will love you." Lindsey stepped into her black strappy sandals. "So, where's Baxter?"

Lindsey noticed the slight frown on her sister's face as Risa waved her hand. "Oh, he stayed in Atlanta. He had some business to attend to."

"You didn't ask him to come, did you."

"I'm not ready for that. After you get married and Dawn is settled—"

"Risa, eventually he's going to find out that Dawn is your daughter. You can't keep your family a secret forever, especially if we all come to your wedding. He'll learn the truth sooner or later. Is that what you want, starting out your marriage with lies?" She thought of Gabe's expression at the park. Thought about the fact that she hadn't confided to Gabe about her inability to have children. No, lies were not going to help her sister.

"Lindsey, I'm not as brave as you are. I know that Baxter expects me to act a certain way. If my past comes up, well, he'll dump me."

"Then he really doesn't love you."

Risa's face slowly turned red. Apparently Lindsey touched a nerve. Especially with facing the truth, which Risa religiously avoided. "You don't know that. You don't know Baxter."

"You're right, I don't. And it doesn't sound like you do, either."

"You don't know what you're talking about." Risa crossed her arms over her chest. The gesture went well with her defiant pout.

"You're right, I don't. I can't say my approach to relationships is any better."

At Lindsey's confession, Risa visibly relaxed.

"Look, I need to get going. It wouldn't look right for the fundraising chair to be late, right? Maybe we can talk more later."

Risa gave a half-nod, not committing either way.

Grabbing her evening bag, Lindsey swept out of the room. Just as she entered the living room of the cottage, Dawn came in through the front door.

"Hey, Mom?"

"What?" both Lindsey and Risa answered in unison. Lindsey turned to catch her sister's matching stunned expression as Dawn ran in from the porch. Her long skirt flew around her ankles, her bright, cherub-like expression missing the exchange brought on by her innocent words. "Mr. Banner is here! He's all dressed up, like you. And Emily has on the dress we all went shopping for." She stopped before Lindsey and gave her a hug. "Think you guys will pick a wedding date tonight?"

Lindsey swallowed hard, not sure how to reply. "I'm sure we'll talk about it."

"Good, because Emily and I have some ideas and we've been writing them down." She took a step back and saw Risa hovering in the doorway. "Oh, hi. I didn't know you were here."

"I came in the back way."

Before the situation became more awkward, the doorbell rang.

"See you later," Risa said quietly as she came up beside Lindsey.

"Later," Lindsey replied, watching her sister leave.

Dawn ran to the front door to let in an excited Emily. The two chattered while Lindsey waited for Gabe to enter. Her stomach twisted. What if he was still upset with her?

Her heart soared as he walked in from outdoors, tall and handsome. She forgot her fears and drank in the sight of him. The tuxedo he wore fit him to a T. He'd gotten his hair trimmed and brushed it off his forehead. His dark tan brought a startling contrast to the whiteness of his shirt. He moved closer and she smelled the tangy cologne she would forever associate with him.

He had to be the most desirable man in the entire world. And he was her date.

He smiled, that amused glint back in his eyes. After the way they parted yesterday, why was he looking at her that way, like he held a secret and he meant to tease her by keeping her in suspense? Or did she dare hope that he'd forgive the actions of two friends, an action that belonged in the past. From the depths of her soul, she pulled out her brightest smile, determined to make this night special for all of them.

"Ready?" Gabe asked.

"As ready as I'll ever be. But Gabe, before we go, I have to ask, are you okay, you know, about our conversation yesterday?"

"Actually, I am. I had time to think about it and realize that was a long time ago. I'm ready to move on."

Lindsey let out a relieved breath.

He grinned. "Don't worry so much. About us, or about tonight's gala. It will be a success."

"I hope so. I've worked so long and hard."

"And hard work always pays off."

"Okay, that makes sense, but . . ."

"You're still nervous."

She nodded.

"Don't be. You're beautiful, Lindsey. I don't know about any other guys, but I won't be able to keep my eyes off you."

She felt herself grow warm at his declaration, telling herself to count her blessings. He was here, with her, by choice.

"As long as we're okay . . ."

"We're better than okay."

He walked over and for the first time she noticed he kept one arm behind his back. He stopped before her, brought his arm around and presented her with a florist box.

She eyed the box, her heart pounding. "What's this?"

"Open it up."

She took the proffered box and slowly opened it. Inside she found a beautiful wrist corsage made of yellow baby roses surrounded by wisps of baby's breath.

"Oh, my," she whispered.

"A little late, but think of this as a gift for the prom." He took the box from her hands and removed the corsage. "Here, let me put it on for you."

She lifted her right arm and he carefully slid it over her hand and settled the roses at her wrist. She lifted it upward toward her nose, inhaling the heady fragrance. As far as she was concerned, the night was an unmitigated success.

Gabe remained by her side, not wanting to let go of her hand. The dreamy expression on her face from his gift set his pulse racing. His small gesture lit up her lovely eyes with delight. And he hadn't even given her the ring yet. Or told her that he loved her. He planned to do both later tonight.

"Okay, ladies. Let's get going. Lindsey has things to take care of before the crowd arrives."

He ushered his future family out to the Lexus, taking his time to be sure Lindsey settled carefully into the car before closing the door.

The girls chattered on the trip into town, but Lindsey stared out the window, occasionally glancing at her corsage. He smiled. From the minute he came up with the idea, he knew she'd melt at his gesture. The only thing that bothered him right now was the emotional distance she put between them. The only way to close the distance would be to sit down and tell her that he'd made his decision to let go of the past. That the note didn't matter, only she did. Once he had the opportunity to tell her, he felt sure things would be right between them.

Soon, they arrived at the historic Half Moon Lodge, nestled into the mountainside. Made of dark wood beams and hearty lumber with a soft patina of age, the rustic structure had been around almost as long as the original settlers. What had started as a shelter for the early pioneers during storms and harsh winters, had became an important part of Paineville history. Soon, it's purpose changed to becoming a layover for settlers moving to different mountain communities, then an all-purpose community facility. It was used as a meeting place, and had now evolved into a beautiful location for wedding receptions, and now, the gala.

Gabe knew Lindsey had spent a lot of time there recently with her team; overseeing the decorating, meeting with the caterers, and putting together a display wall outlining the history of the Paineville Library, as well as explaining Lindsey's literacy program.

He'd missed her last night when he stopped in to visit her, but he'd seen the fruits of her hard work and pride swelled in him. He'd heard her talk about the literacy program, but he'd never realized her hard work and how much the community benefited by the tireless hours she put into this labor of love. More than ever, he realized just how lucky he was and what a terrific woman he was going to marry. They may have hit a rough patch, but he knew they could work it out. They had to.

The waiters, dressed in subtle, elegant uniforms, set out the final touches to the tables and readied the food. Actors dressed in costume as couples from famous works of literature—such as Romeo and Juliet, Gatsby and Daisy, Cathy and Heathcliff, Scarlet and Rhett—gathered together for a final briefing before the guests arrived. They would roam around the crowd tonight, encouraging folks to read their favorite books, to experience how a book could come to life, just as their characters had.

Gabe sauntered up beside Lindsey and wrapped his arm around her waist.

"You've done a great job, Linds."

She beamed at him. "I hope everyone else thinks so."

He leaned close, breathing in her floral scent and brushed his lips over her soft cheek. "They do."

She leaned into him and he felt her sigh.

"This feels right, you know that?"

She gazed up and searched his eyes. "We're okay?"

"We're better than okay." He turned her and circled her in his arms. "You threw me for a loop, but I thought about it. A lot of things make sense. I always thought you had a crush on me, so when Cindy showed up at the park, I was a little confused." He smiled, full of fond memories. "I wouldn't change what happened, but I'm also glad you're in my life."

Deciding this was the perfect moment, Gabe reached into

his jacket pocket and extracted a blue velvet jeweler's box. He opened it to show Lindsey the diamond solitaire sparkling inside.

"Oh, Gabe, it's gorgeous. I don't know what to say."

"Say you'll wear my ring."

He swallowed hard as he watched the tears misting her eyes. He hadn't realized her reaction would affect him so deeply, but it did. In a good way.

She nodded, her left hand splayed over her heart. He took the ring from the box, then took her hand and slowly slid the ring on her finger. He stared into her eyes, seeing the joy, and yes, reservations, there.

"This is for always, Linds. And just in case you're wondering, I'm marrying you because I love you, not because of your sister's crazy plan."

Her eyes grew wide, then with a sob, she threw her arms around his neck. He hugged her back, holding her snugly against him. He could get used to this. Holding her close anytime he chose to, especially once they were married.

"I never thought I'd hear those words from you."

"It kind of crept up on me. You slowly worked your way into my heart."

She smiled up at him, joy radiating from her.

"I was thinking Memorial Day weekend."

She pulled back from his embrace. "Excuse me?"

"The girls want us to set a date. You've got the ring. So, why wait? We're not kids, and the girls really want us to be a family. What do you think?"

He found himself holding his breath, waiting for her answer. He didn't think waiting on any one decision could make his chest hurt like it did now.

She gazed at the ring and a concerned frown wrinkled her brow. "That's only a month away. Think we can pull it off?"

"Between both of our families? Oh, yeah, we can do it."

"So, it's official?" she asked in a soft tone.

"It's official."

Not able to hold back any longer, he lowered his head and touched his lips to hers. Soft and gentle, it started with the promise of a future together, but quickly changed to deep and probing with the anticipation of a lifetime spent on practicing the art of kissing.

Lindsey returned his attention, sending his temperature rising. Her pliant lips tasted like heaven, the combination of innocence and passion was heady stuff. Gabe couldn't remember the last time he'd felt so strong, so intently male. Lindsey brought out those qualities in him, made him feel whole and ready to take the next step in his life. The idea of kissing Lindsey for the remainder of his days, and having her return the gesture, made his pulse race. He kissed her more boldly, thoroughly.

At the sound of a not-so-discrete cough somewhere around him, Gabe reluctantly broke the kiss, all the time wishing they were somewhere private. Instead, he let Lindsey slowly surface from his attentions before he embarrassed her by kissing her senseless in public.

He looked up to spy Ty and a very pregnant Casey ambling toward them. "Hey, bro. I think there's some statute about public displays of affection."

Gabe smiled. He'd told Ty something similar the first time he'd met Casey. Ty had been kissing her at the time, in the town square.

"Now I know why you ignored me when I caught you and Casey stuck in that liplock."

Ty laughed loudly and pulled Casey to his side. Her wan smile lacked its usual sparkle and her pale skin alarmed him.

"You okay?" Gabe asked.

"Just a little tired. I didn't want to miss Lindsey's party. It's my last shot at socializing until the baby comes."

"I tried to get her to stay home," Ty told them, "but you know Casey when her mind is set. C'mon, darlin', let's go find a place to sit down."

"Wait," Casey exclaimed, grabbing Lindsey's hand. "Is that what I think it is?"

With a shy smile, Lindsey flashed her newly adorned ring finger. "Yes."

"I thought so. How wonderful, you guys."

While Lindsey and Casey discussed the engagement, Ty lifted an eyebrow at Gabe. "How on earth did she notice?"

Gabe laughed. "Must be a woman thing. They have radar for this stuff."

Ty clapped his brother on the back. "Congrats, bro. 'Bout time you decided to join the land of the living."

Gabe glanced over at Lindsey and his chest swelled. "She's worth it."

The women rejoined them and Ty took his wife's hand, leading her to a waiter with a tray of hors d'oeuvres. Casey shook her head and pointed to the nearest table with chairs.

Lindsey took Gabe's hand in hers, her worried gaze following Casey. "Do you think she'll be okay?"

"Yeah," he replied with a sheepish grin. "Once the baby is born."

The mayor came by with the new Miss Georgia, a Paineville girl, to congratulate Lindsey on the apparent success of the gala. Gabe pretty much lost sight of Lindsey for an hour. By the time she finally came back to spend time with him, Casey announced she had to be taken to the hospital.

"It's time," she told Ty while she pressed her hand against her swollen stomach.

Gabe glanced over at his panic-stricken brother and took control of the situation. "Sorry Linds, we have to leave."

"Do you need me to do anything?"

He thought about it for a split second. "Yeah, come with us to the hospital." He saw her smile slip at his words. "Sorry, I can't ask you that. You've got your award—"

"This is more important, Gabe. I want to be with you and your family."

Her agreement lightened the weight he hadn't realized sat on his shoulders. "You're sure?"

She hugged him and kissed him on the cheek. "I'm sure."

After Lindsey informed her family she'd be leaving with Gabe, he managed to get everyone to the hospital. The girls stayed with Lindsey's mother, but Gabe promised to call Emily as soon as anything happened. Marilyn and Dusty brought Ruby Sue with them.

Once Casey and Ty disappeared into the birthing room, all everyone could do was wait. The Banner family painted a strange picture, everyone dressed in fancy gowns and tuxedos, milling around the sterile waiting room.

Gabe ran a hand through his hair as he joined Lindsey. "Now I know what the family went through when Em was born."

Lindsey grinned. "She was well worth the wait."

Gabe sat beside her on the plastic molded chair and draped his arm over his shoulder. "Yes, she was."

She rested her head on his shoulder. "Ruby Sue is so excited she can't stand herself."

"She's wanted another great-grandchild for a long time now." He gazed down at Lindsey. "Hey, I'm sorry we didn't get to announce our news tonight. And you missed the most important part of the gala, your award."

"In light of the miracle of birth, I think we can tell people another time."

"You sure you're not disappointed?"

She held out the ring so they both could admire it. "Positive."

Gabe didn't know how much time went by before a jubilant Ty came rushing down the hallway. "It's a boy!" He hauled Ruby Sue up into his arms and swung her around.

"Put me down, boy, before you break a hip."

"I won't break your hip."

"I'm not talking about mine, I mean yours!"

Ty set her down, bending over so she could kiss him on the cheek. "How's that wife of yours doing?"

"Casey is fine. Tired, but she's a trouper."

"And the baby?" Gabe asked.

"He came a little early, but the doctor checked him out and says he's great." Ty walked over and hugged Gabe around the neck. "Do you believe it? I'm a dad."

Gabe laughed, and hugged his brother in return, understanding the joy that so filled a man when his child came into the world. "Yeah, buddy, you're a dad."

By this time, Ruby Sue demanded to see her grandbaby, so the group headed toward the nursery. Lindsey hung back.

"You know," he told her, "I didn't think I wanted to have any more kids. Emily is a handful all by herself. But now that we're getting married, I can't wait to have a bunch of our own." Gabe held out his hand. "C'mon. Let's go see the baby."

She took his hand and smiled, but he noticed a hint of sadness in her eyes.

"You okay?"

"Yes. Sorry, I started thinking about when Risa delivered Dawn. None of us were there at the time."

He lifted her chin and planted a brief kiss on her lips. "I'm glad you're here with the family now."

"Thanks for including me."

"Of course, I wouldn't want you to be anywhere else but by my side."

Chapter Fourteen

Lindsey knocked and asked through Risa's door, "Hey, mind if I come in?"

"No. C'mon in."

Lindsey pushed open the bedroom door in her parent's house to find her sister dressed in her silky pajamas, pulling down the bed covers. "How did everything go with Casey and the baby?"

"Great. Ruby Sue now has a beautiful baby boy to spoil." Lindsey laughed to herself, remembering the look of rapture on the older woman's lined face. "Mother and child are doing fine."

Risa smiled. "We were all thinking about them."

"Turns out the baby was a little early."

"I'm glad everything worked out." Risa climbed onto, the bed and sat cross-legged, leaning against the headboard, a pillow held against her mid-section. Lindsey noticed she seemed a bit subdued.

"I came over to check on the girls and Mom told me you wowed the mayor at the Gala. Not an easy feat."

Risa shrugged.

"Thanks for filling in for me."

"No big deal." Her expression grew serious. "After the mayor presented the award, Alanna got up to speak. She talked all about your vision for the literacy program. I have to say, I'm impressed."

Lindsey took a seat at the end of the bed, smoothing her long skirt. "It's something I'm really passionate about. When I started tutoring children, I realized that many of their parents needed help too. That's when I got involved in adult literacy and it just snowballed from there. Anyway, thanks for filling in for me."

"I still can't believe you left with Gabe and missed getting the award yourself."

"It was more important to be with him."

Risa shook her head. "Why sacrifice your night for him?"

"Because I love him. And that's what you do for people you love. You sacrifice. You make a way for things to work out."

"Like your marrying Gabe."

Lindsey looked away from her. "It may not be the smartest thing I've ever done, considering I haven't told Gabe I can't have children but, yeah, I'm marrying him to make sure everything works out for him and the girls."

"What about you?"

"I'm the optimist, remember?" Lindsey forced a smile. "Gabe is what I want. What I've always wanted."

"I know that." Risa shifted. "It must be nice, you know, to be passionate about something. Anything."

Lindsey looked at her sister, at the lost, little-girl pose and helplessness in her wide eyes. Suddenly she felt like the older sister. That was her, the responsible sister. The one to make things right. Even if it meant getting married because Risa couldn't deal with reality.

"Risa, can I ask you something?"

"Sure."

"Tonight, when I saw Casey holding the baby with such a look of awe on her face, I couldn't help but wonder what you felt when you had Dawn."

Risa blinked. "It's been a long time since I thought about it."

"Humor me."

She sighed. "You know I never took the idea of motherhood seriously. So when Dawn finally arrived, I held this small baby in my arms and realized I was in no way ready for this kind of responsibility. I mean, look at my life. I was throwing temper tantrums when I was ten. Still do." She laughed sadly.

"I've always expected the world to revolve around me. When the first good-looking guy showed up in town, I saw him as a ticket to freedom. I never thought I'd end up becoming a mother when I barely understood what it meant to be a wife. Then Dawn's father left and I knew she was better off here with an entire family to raise her. I knew she'd be better off with you."

"So that's it. You just decided to bring her to us and leave, never looking back?"

"I know what you've thought of me all these years; what kind of mother dumps her child off with relatives? But really, Lindsey, how could I stay and watch her grow up knowing I couldn't take care of her."

"You never tried. Don't you think Dawn wonders what it would be like to have her real Mom in her life, instead of this elusive person who drifts in and out of her life?"

"It's too late for that."

"No. It's not. Tonight, after seeing Casey with the baby, I realized that Dawn deserves more from us. All of us. She needs to know her mother, her natural mother. She needs to know *you*, Risa. I love her as if she were my own daughter, but that's not the point."

Risa's surprise showed in her eyes. "But you've always taken care of her. Especially when you learned you couldn't have children of your own. You've given Dawn the emotional support she needs, been her real mother."

"You can do the same. It all comes down to love. I know you can love. You wouldn't have saddled me with your crazy ultimatum if you didn't love Dawn so much. You want the best for her. Only you've gone about it the wrong way. It's not me who needs to be married for Dawn to have a complete family. She needs you and Baxter in her life. That's why you need to tell him the truth. Forget about Risa for just this once and think about Dawn."

In the dim lighting of the room, Lindsey saw tears glisten in Risa's eyes. "I really don't want to blow this."

"Then you need to take the first step. Tell the truth." She knew she had to tell Gabe about her medical problem. And she prayed he'd forgive her for not speaking up sooner. That he wouldn't reject her.

She touched Risa's arm and spoke to herself as much as her sister. "No matter how hard it is, no matter the outcome, Baxter will appreciate knowing the truth."

"I don't know if I can do this," Risa whispered.

A thought suddenly occurred to Lindsey. For so long Risa had called the shots, made the demands. Now Lindsey had a chance to prove her point to Risa, in a way Risa could understand.

"You gave me an ultimatum and I did it. Now it's your turn. Right now, *you're* the one on a deadline. Because one way or another, Baxter will find out. Deep down, I think you know this." She held up her left hand to show Risa the diamond solitaire Gabe had slipped on her finger tonight.

"Come the last weekend in May, we'll be getting married. You have until then to tell Baxter about Dawn."

The night of the wedding rehearsal came more quickly than Lindsey had anticipated. She stood in the back of the 100-year-old church, wearing a navy-blue, wraparound dress, worrying about how she looked after going through another agonizing makeover session with her mother, while both families of the bride and groom mingled up front. Gabe stood tall beside his brother and best man. He looked so handsome, dressed in a dark suit, so sure and solid that Lindsey had to blink back tears.

What on earth was she doing here? She still hadn't told Gabe they'd never have children. She'd been so busy, so caught up in the wedding preparations that she hadn't had the time. Or taken the time. *Sorry, Gabe, can't have kids. Well, he'd say, in that case, we can't get married.* She couldn't bear that.

It figured. Gabe finally falls for her, really wants to marry her, and she can't reveal the one secret that would destroy their relationship. Lindsey had loved Gabe for so long, she expected this night and tomorrow's ceremony to be the most wonderful time of her life.

Instead, she was miserable.

What a mess.

The door opened and Risa rushed in, followed by a tall, distinguished looking man. After much thought, Lindsey had asked her sister to serve as maid of honor. Risa accepted with a whoop, then cried as she hugged Lindsey, telling her how much this gesture meant to her.

"Lindsey, what are you doing here in the back of the church?" Risa asked. "Shouldn't you be up front with Gabe?"

"Just fighting pre-wedding jitters."

"You? Jitters? This is what you've waited for your entire life."

"Right." Lindsey didn't want to get into her insecurities right now. If she did, the enormity of what she was doing would no doubt make her think twice and run out the door.

Risa beamed up at the man standing beside her. "Lindsey, I want you to meet my fiancé, Baxter."

"I've heard nothing but good things about you," Baxter told Lindsey, shaking her trembling, clammy hand.

"Thanks." She glanced at her sister, rising her brow in question.

"I took your advice. I sat down with Baxter and told him all about the family. All about me and Dawn."

He put his arm around her shoulder, hugging a beaming Risa closer. "I can't believe she thought I would break up with her because of Dawn. If anything, I love her more for making the difficult decision to finally confide in me."

Lindsey's stomach dropped and she had a hard time breathing.

Risa stared adoringly up at Baxter. "It was rough at first. But we talked and talked and you were right." She smiled at Lindsey. "We do love each other. Telling the truth was the best thing I've ever done."

"So, now what?"

"I know this is your night to rehearse for the wedding tomorrow, but I'd hoped to introduce Baxter to the family and announce our engagement."

Lindsey swallowed hard. "What about Dawn?"

"Um, I think we should talk about that later."

"No, I think we should talk about it now."

Before Risa had a chance to answer, Gabe joined them in the foyer, concern slanting his eyebrows. "Everything all right?" He pierced Lindsey with his gaze. "We're ready when you are."

Lindsey turned to him and smiled nervously. "Please, just give me five minutes."

"Okay. I'll tell the family." Gabe backed away, reluctance in every step.

Lindsey returned her attention to her sister. "What about Dawn?"

"Baxter and I decided that we should be a family. I was going to wait until after your wedding to tell you and talk to Dawn."

"Risa, my whole wedding is because I wanted to keep Dawn." Lindsey took a step backward. Now who was being disingenuous?

"But the other night, when we talked, you made it sound like I should try to be a mother to Dawn." Confusion wrinkled Risa's brow. "Isn't that what you meant?"

Is that what she meant? She thought she did at the time. But now, Risa was making an adult decision and Lindsey didn't know what to think. She stared at Risa, the walls falling in around her. Here she stood, ready to marry Gabe tomorrow, to keep the family together, when she might lose Dawn anyway. The things that seemed so clear just days ago now seemed blurry.

"Lindsey?"

She turned blindly at Gabe's voice. How could she tell him that her world was falling apart? Nothing in her life was turning out like she'd hoped. Nothing.

"I have to leave," she whispered to no one in particular.

As she started for the doors, Gabe grabbed her arm. "Lindsey—"

She took a deep breath and shook off his grasp. Heart breaking, she looked at him through tear-filled eyes. "I'm sorry Gabe, I can't marry you."

* * *

Lindsey stared out into the darkness of the parking lot, trying to remember where she'd parked her car. Her heavy heart pounded in her chest and her damp lashes created a rainbow effect when she looked at a light in the distance. Miserable wasn't a good enough description for her current condition.

Gabe's calm voice startled her out of her pity party. "Want to tell me what's going on?"

"It's over, Gabe. The game is over."

"I don't think so."

"I can't marry you."

"And I deserve an explanation."

She hugged her arms across her stomach. Words failed her. She stared at him, mute.

"C'mon."

He led her to the Lexus and helped her inside. They endured thick silence for long moments. Sick with worry, she sat immobile in the passenger seat, waiting for the inevitable conversation.

"I guess now would be a good time to tell me why you can't marry me."

Fresh tears assaulted her again. "I can't marry you under false pretenses."

"Come again?"

"That man with Risa is her fiancé." She told him about Risa's fear of telling Baxter the truth and the conversation that had just taken place in the church. "Risa and Baxter want to make a new family, with Dawn. She's taking Dawn away. Dawn is part of the reason we're getting married."

"You think we're getting married only because of Dawn?"

"And Emily. They need a solid family. We can give them that."

"Lindsey, I think there's more to what's going on here."

"No. I'm tired of thinking there is. Tired of thinking I could tell you . . ."

"Tell me what? I think I'm missing something here."

"Gabe. You're a smart guy. Without Dawn, we'd only be part of a family. And without Dawn . . ." She choked on the words.

"What do you mean?"

"I haven't been completely honest with you."

"Yeah, you told me about the note."

"No, it's something else." She dragged in a ragged breath. "I can't have children, Gabe. The doctor told me years ago. That's why Dawn is so precious to me, why I've put up with Risa's stuff for so long. Dawn is my only chance to be a mother. But not at your expense. That's why I can't marry you. You deserve more."

Gabe stared out the window, while she held her breath and waited for the look of disappointment when he faced her again.

"I should have told you sooner, but I couldn't make myself do it and risk having you leave me. But it isn't right to saddle you with my problems and I've done that since you came back to town. I know how hurt and angry you were when I didn't tell you about the note, so I wouldn't blame you for hating me for keeping something this important from you."

Gabe turned to face her, but the fresh tears in her eyes kept her from reading his expression. Instead of blasting her, to her surprise, he slid over and took her in his arms. "How could you think I'd turn you away over something you have no control over?"

"I've lived with the truth for so long, I guess I've convinced myself no one would want me."

His hands on her upper arms, Gabe set her back to look directly into her eyes. "I want you."

"But—"

"I'm surprised by your news, I'll admit that. But that doesn't change the fact that I love you. That I want us to be a family."

She stared up at him, hope filling her heart.

"We can deal with not having children. We have Emily and Dawn."

"But for how long?"

"Are you sure about Risa? Did she actually say she was taking Dawn?"

Did she say that? Lindsey thought hard about Risa's words. "She said they were going to talk to Dawn."

"That's a lot different than Risa taking her."

"It's only a matter of time. You know how Risa is when she puts her mind to something."

"She did put her mind to something, to see that Dawn has a good home. And Dawn will have that, with us."

"How can you be so sure it's that simple?"

"Because despite her actions, Risa knows her shortcomings. She hasn't dealt with them very well, but she knows deep down, you're the best mother for Dawn. Even if she marries, she's smart enough to know that she can't replace the bond between you and Dawn. And I think she's finally learned not to try."

Lindsey shook her head, not convinced.

Gabe folded her in the warmth of his arms again. "Where is the happy-go-lucky Lindsey I became reacquainted with months ago?"

"She's confused and tired and worried about everything."

Gabe chuckled. "That's a tall order. Trust me, Linds, you can't control everything. I've tried. It doesn't work. You have to have faith that everything will work out. That our love is strong enough to get us through any problems life throws our way."

She sighed, still wishing for the magic answer.

"I want to show you something." He set her back in her seat then started the car and drove for a few blocks, stopping at the old Olsen house.

She pushed open the door and stepped onto the concrete driveway, feeling a little more in control now that they were away from the church. "Why are we here? Aren't you still working on this house?"

He took her hand and led her up the path, his key ready to unlock the front door. He pulled her over the threshold, flipping on the foyer light switch to illuminate the dark house.

"I think now is a good time to give you your wedding present."

She followed him into the empty living room where he stopped dead center and extended his arms. "Welcome to the new Banner house."

Her heart flipped in surprise. "What? Is Ruby Sue moving?"

"No."

"What does this have to do with my present?"

"I know how much you love this house and after all the work Ty and I did to remodel, I couldn't pass up the chance to buy it."

She looked around, looked at Gabe. "This is my present?"

"Yeah. It's too big to wrap."

"Oh, Gabe, you shouldn't have."

"The location is perfect, away from our families, but close enough to visit. The girls can walk to school and it's close to the library. And, there's the addition on the east side of the house. I was thinking I could use it as my office when I open my law practice. That is, after I get my Georgia license."

"You've decided to practice again? Gabe, that's wonderful."

"Yeah. I've come to learn in the past weeks that I do miss helping people. And being immersed in the law. It's a lot tidier than sawdust."

His smile dimmed as he waited for her reaction. "So, what do you think about all this?"

Still, she didn't speak, just gazed around the big, open room, longing reflected in her eyes.

Gabe knelt on one knee before her and took the hand with the engagement ring into his. "Linds, I want to marry you. For all the right reasons. You've taught me that it's possible to love more than once in a lifetime. This house is getting a second chance, and so are we. It's a physical reminder of our love, our commitment, our family. It's what you've always wanted."

She laughed and wiped at the tears wetting her cheeks before throwing her arms around Gabe's neck. He stood, holding her tight, and kissed her. She met his kiss with a deep sense of need that matched his.

Gabe broke the kiss. "You deserve this house and more. You deserve all the love every woman wants from a man. Not as an old friend, but in the romantic, Cupid-arrow-shooting, bells and whistles, heart-pounding kind of way. I'm that man for you, Linds. Always and forever."

"Even if I can't have a baby?"

"No contingencies."

"And if I can't keep Dawn?"

"Just unconditional love."

All the tension of the past weeks drained from her, leaving only the strong love she had for Gabe. "How can I refuse?"

"So you'll marry me? Will you be my wife and love me for the rest of our days?"

Lindsey's heart swelled with joy. "Yes, Gabe Banner, I will marry you."

Gabe let out a whoop of unrestrained emotion, then lifted her in his arms to twirl them around the empty room. She held on for dear life, and that's where she wanted to stay, in Gabe's arms forever.

"Then what are we waiting for? There's a church full of people waiting for us to share our vows." He chuckled. "We don't want to disappoint them, especially after all their hard work to get us together."

He slowed and let Lindsey slide her feet to the floor, love lighting her eyes. "Then let's get back to the church," she said with total confidence in her voice. "This time, love is all we need."

Epilogue

Seven Months Later

Lindsey watched the tired, but happy family in Ruby Sue's parlor open their Christmas presents. Marilyn had come home from the hospital two days before, bringing with her Ruby Sue's second great-grandson. Ruby Sue beamed from ear to ear at all the family gathered in her cozy house.

The entire Summer family showed up and joined the happy occasion while pitching in to help. Dorothea cooked up a big breakfast and the lingering scent of bacon and freshly brewed coffee filled the house. The girls dove into their presents, helping baby Jordan, who didn't know quite what to make of all the commotion. He kept looking up at his smiling daddy, Ty, who held his chubby, dark-haired son securely on his lap.

Gabe came up behind Lindsey, where she leaned against the banister to watch the merriment, and hugged her. "Holding up, okay?"

"Enjoying every minute of it. We haven't had this exciting a Christmas in years."

"If this family continues to grow, Christmas will always be exciting. Chaotic, but exciting."

She turned in his arms and hugged him close, sighing. Seven months of wedded bliss. She didn't think they could be any happier. And she hadn't even given him his Christmas present yet.

The doorbell rang. Laurel Ann opened the door to usher in Risa and her husband Baxter. Everyone called out greetings while Dawn rushed over for a hug.

Warmth filled Lindsey's heart. After the wedding, Lindsey, Gabe, Risa, Baxter and Dawn sat down for a serious talk. Dawn listened, weighed the consequences and came up with a solution everyone could live with. Dawn needed time to get to know Risa before they could have a real mother/daughter relationship. And her bond with Lindsey went so deeply, that she decided to stay with the new Banner family, visiting Risa from time to time for long weekends. The decision went over well, especially with her new step-sister, Emily, who was invited to come on many long weekends if she wished. Risa seemed to take her new role in Dawn's life seriously. Lindsey figured it had a lot to do with Baxter, who was a good influence on her sister. All in all, things had turned out for the best.

Marilyn came down the stairs, holding baby Brandon, a sleepy grin on her face. When she spied Lindsey nearby, she walked straight to her and placed the baby in Lindsey's arms.

"Would you mind holding him for a bit. I want to get some of that breakfast before the men eat it all."

Lindsey laughed and gathered Brandon close. "My pleasure."

As she cooed and hummed to the baby, Gabe stood at her side, gazing down at his nephew. "It never ceases to amaze me what a miracle children are."

"I know. I can hardly wait to have our baby."

"Linds, don't get too ahead of yourself. The doctor said it might take a while to have our family with that new medicine you're taking."

"I'm not worried," she replied with a satisfied smile. "Nine months should do nicely."

Gabe's gaze grew quizzical.

"I think its time to give you your Christmas present."

Lindsey handed Brandon to Casey and took Gabe's hand in hers, leading him into the foyer where they grabbed their jackets from the wall hooks and moved out to the front porch.

"What's going on?" Gabe asked, rubbing his hands together in the brisk December air. The endearing look of bewilderment reminded her of why she fell in love with him so long ago. "You're not upset about being around the babies, are you? The doctor told us to be patient."

"I know, I went to see him yesterday."

He went still. "Are you okay?"

"I'm fine. Excellent."

"Okay, tell me."

She took a deep breath, afraid she might burst with the news. "We're going to have our own baby."

Gabe took a step back and shook his head. "Wait, how is that possible? You haven't been taking the new medication for very long."

"It's nothing short of a Christmas miracle."

"My God," Gabe breathed, then took her in his arms and swung her around and around.

She laughed. "Gabe, you're making me dizzy."

He gently set her down. "I can't believe this."

"Well, believe."

He took her face into his hands, brushing his lips over hers. "I didn't think I could be any happier than I am. Thank you, Lindsey. Just a year ago I'd have sworn I was going to live a solitary life, never practice law again, and wallow in the past. But you changed everything. I love you."

"I love you, Gabe. And this baby is just the beginning of all the wonderful things for this family."

Still smiling, he took her hand. "Let's go inside and share the good news."

"Lead on."

Lindsey breathed in the crisp winter air, fulfilled and content with her life, and followed Gabe inside. After removing the bulky winter jackets, they stood on the edge of the parlor, Gabe's arm around her shoulder, drinking in the scene of the big, loud, loving family before sharing the baby news.

"I have to say," Gabe said with pride in his voice, "the Banners have come a long way."

Lindsey slipped her arm around his waist. "And the next generation will be even better. We have a lot to look forward to."

He kissed the top of her head. "I wouldn't want to share this time with anyone but you."